O9-CFT-021

TAKE ME WITH YOU WHEN YOU GO

Also by David Levithan

Boy Meets Boy
The Realm of Possibility
Are We There Yet?
Wide Awake
How They Met, and Other Stories
Love Is the Higher Law
The Lover's Dictionary
Every Day
Two Boys Kissing
Another Day
Someday
19 Love Songs
The Mysterious Disappearance of Aidan S. (as told to his brother)

Also by Jennifer Niven

All the Bright Places
Holding Up the Universe
Breathless
The Ice Master
Ada Blackjack
Velva Jean Learns to Drive
Velva Jean Learns to Fly
Becoming Clementine
American Blonde

TAKE ME WITH YOU WHEN YOU GO

DAVID LEVITHAN

AND

JENNIFER NIVEN

ALFRED A. KNOPF
NEW YORK

THIS IS A BORZOI BOOK PUBLISHED BY ALFRED A. KNOPF

Visit us on the Web! GetUnderlined.com

Educators and librarians, for a variety of teaching tools, visit us at RHTeachersLibrarians.com

Library of Congress Cataloging-in-Publication Data is available upon request.
ISBN 978-0-525-58099-7 (trade) — ISBN 978-0-525-58100-0 (lib. bdg.) —
ISBN 978-0-525-58101-7 (ebook)

The text of this book is set in 11-point Maxime Pro.
Interior design by Cathy Bobak

Printed in the United States of America
August 2021
10 9 8 7 6 5 4 3 2 1

First Edition

With gratitude to all the indie booksellers, especially everyone at Little City Books (my local that got me through a pandemic), Books of Wonder (for almost two decades of support to date), and Avid Bookshop (my local that I don't live anywhere near).

—D.L.

For Joe and Angelo, brothers of my heart. I love you more than Harry Styles and ABBA and popcorn. And words—I love you more than words.

—J.N.

As far as you take me
That's where I believe
—The Smashing Pumpkins,
"Porcelina of the Vast Oceans"

Subject: You. Missing.
From: e89898989@ymail.com
To: b989898989@ymail.com
Date: Mon 25 Mar 12:12 EST

Dear Bea,

I am not mad at you. I don't blame you. But I do think you owe me an explanation.

I know you're gone. We all know you're gone. I think from the moment Mom went into your room and found it the way you left it, we knew. What an exquisite *fuck you* to her and Darren—a perfectly made bed. Like it had never been slept in. Like you'd never been here at all. How many times have they yelled at you to make that bed? How many times have you refused? (Hint: The answer to both questions is the same number.) And now: You left everything smooth and blank.

No note. No word.

I know. I looked.

I wasn't the one who found your room like that. I was sitting at the kitchen table, trying to eat cereal in a way that wouldn't annoy Darren. Suddenly Mom was screaming your name. Again and again, angry at first, then something else—maybe ten percent scared. (It maxed out there, about ten percent.) I'll admit I didn't think much of it, since no morning would be complete without you two fighting. Darren didn't look up from his toast either. But then Mom came storming into the kitchen and launched right into me—*Where is your sister? Tell me right now where she is.*

If I were you, I would have responded with something like "How the fuck should I know?" or "Isn't it a little early for this shit, Mom?" But it's a well-established fact that I am not you, so immediately I was like, "I don't know I don't know I don't know—what's going onnnnnnn?" Sounding guilty as I tried so hard to sound innocent. Then she turned to Darren and was like, "She's gone," and he was like, "How the hell can she be gone?"

As an answer, we took a family trip up to your room. That's when I saw your bed and thought, *Oh, wow. She's taken off.*

I wasn't going to say anything more than that, but they saw me looking around and Darren was on me in a flash, asking what was missing. I pointed out that your backpack wasn't anywhere in sight, and that your schoolbooks were now stacked next to your garbage pail. (Nice touch.) Also, the biggest shock, your phone was abandoned on your dresser. Presumably so we couldn't use it to track you.

Mom and Darren acted like insider knowledge was required to make this observation, so the interrogation resumed. I didn't crack, though. Or wait—I guess I *did* crack. But they quickly saw there wasn't anything behind the crack. You'd left me empty too.

They might have kept on me—there wasn't anything else for them to do, or at least nothing else that was occurring to them—

but at that moment we were jolted by a honk outside. And I'll admit—even though it didn't really surprise me to find you were gone, it surprised the heck out of me to have Joe in front of our house, coming to pick you up. Because that meant you'd left him too.

I probably don't need to describe the ambush that followed. Darren dragging poor Joe out of the car, into the kitchen. Sitting him down, asking him hundreds of questions. And Joe sitting there, it dawning on him that his girlfriend has vanished. You are his life, Bea. You know that. And of all people, *Darren* was telling him that his life had walked out the door. Buh-bye.

Even though Darren yelled at Joe to look at him, only him, Joe kept looking over to me, begging me to tell him this wasn't really happening, that I had a secret message from you, the coordinates of a meeting place where you'd be waiting.

All I could do was shake my head.

Eventually, Mom and Darren were satisfied by Joe's cluelessness. And you know what? The fact that Joe was in the dark pissed them off more. Like they were outraged at how unfair you were being to him, as if they've always been the biggest Joe fans in the world. And in fairness, they probably do like him better than they like either you or me. But that's not exactly an achievement.

Mom actually said to Joe, "Now you see what a liar she can be," as if they were on the same side, as if she was giving him some motherly advice. I didn't get it at all. But, of course, from the moment Mom started dating Darren, I gave up on figuring her out. And figuring out Darren is way too easy, and not very helpful. When things don't go his way, he yells. As you know.

I politely mentioned that it was time to go to school, so I needed to run upstairs and get my stuff. I felt bad about leaving Joe alone with Mom and Darren, but there didn't seem to be any way around it.

The minute I got to my room, I knew exactly where to look. I'm guessing you thought it would take me longer, but it didn't. You know exactly what I found. And what I didn't find.

Look, I don't blame you for taking the money. I'm not at all surprised that you took the money. In fact, I'm going to confess to you that I have more than one hiding place. You knew about the hiding place I told you about, and I never put anything in there that I wasn't okay with you stealing. (I'm not going to call it *borrowing,* although I'm sure that's the way you want me to think of it. I am not expecting any of it back.)

The big question, as I was lifting out the tray of baseball cards, wasn't whether you'd robbed your little brother. It was whether you'd left me something in return.

And you had. This email address.

I'll admit, I didn't even know there was such a thing as ymail. I will make sure no one else knows about this address, and (as you see) I've made up my own return address, only for you. I understand the rules of engagement here. If you'd left without giving me any way to contact you, I wouldn't have ever forgiven you. Ever. But this is okay, I think. As long as you tell me what happened.

Mom and Darren were too busy asking Joe questions to notice me slipping back into the kitchen. To Joe's credit, he was asking questions right back—had they called the police? Had they tried Sloane? Was either of their cars missing?

That last question sent Darren flying from the room, with a look that made it clear he would hold Joe personally responsible if either of the cars was gone. While he checked, Mom said that no, nobody was going to call the police. Beatrix wasn't *abducted.* She wasn't *in danger.* Or if she was in danger, it was her own damn fault.

"We have to get to school," I repeated.

But we weren't going to be cleared to go until Darren was back, saying the cars were safe in the garage. I didn't point out that both sets of keys were sitting on the kitchen counter, which would have saved him a trip.

Joe and I were free to go. We didn't say anything as we walked to the car. We were still afraid Mom and Darren might hear us. It was only when we were safe in the car and I was putting on my seat belt that Joe asked, "Is she really gone?"

And I had to say, yeah, it sure looked like it.

I was mad at you then. Because Joe was trembling. He didn't want me to see him cry. He didn't want to be that guy, not in his own car. But there we were, me sitting in the seat that was always yours. It was like you'd sent me to break up with him, and it didn't matter that you'd dumped me too. Because Joe was the one you were supposed to take along and didn't. It's clear you didn't even ask. I'm not quite sure what he did to deserve that.

I didn't tell him about the email address. Not even when he asked if I knew how to find you. Blood is thicker than water, I suppose. It can also leave a much crueler stain.

We clung to the hope that Sloane would know something, that you'd left some instructions with her. Maybe you were over at her house, waiting for us to find you there. Joe and I tried calling and texting her, but there wasn't any response. With me, I could almost understand—it wouldn't have been out of the question for Mom and Darren to commandeer my phone to track you down. But Joe's calls? I had no idea why she wasn't answering those.

I tried to reassure Joe, telling him you'd run away before, that you'd called it "taking a break," never really going that far. Like the time you got that hotel room in Columbus and crashed that forensics convention until one of the advisors complained you were distracting his team.

I thought this news would make Joe feel better, but he'd never heard any of these stories before, and that only made him feel like more of a heel. I was accidentally emphasizing how little he knew you. Which was odd, because I would've thought he knew you better than I did, for all the time you've spent with him these past couple years.

It's possible I wasn't very convincing when I told him about how you always came back. Because those other times didn't feel like this time. I don't know how to explain it. I saw that bed and knew you were planning to be gone for good. The fact that you'd cleaned out my hiding place confirmed it. You wouldn't have done that unless you really, really needed to, right?

Joe and I got to school, and I was convinced that we knew something that nobody else did—not yet, at least. Everyone was wandering around thinking you were still with us, still a part of the school. *Yeah,* I can imagine you saying, *like they paid so much attention to me while I was there.* But some people did. Joe said he'd look for Sloane, and I said I'd do the same, even though from my freshman vantage point it was going to be harder to track down a senior. I'm sure some detective would ask, "Well, what about looking for *Bea* when you got to school?" But neither of us seriously thought you'd be here. Of all the places in the world, this is the last place you'd escape to.

Terrence was waiting for me at my locker as usual. And I kissed him hello as usual. He asked me how I was doing . . . as usual. And I thought: *This is where it starts. If I tell someone else, that's when the new reality begins.* I wanted to lie to him. But at the same time, if our family has taught me anything, it's that lies will come back to haunt you, and that people are more forgiving up front than if they find out later you've been lying all along. Seeing what you just did to Joe made me want to avoid doing anything like it to Terrence. So I told him the short version. I made it sound less final than it probably is. But I didn't pretend it wasn't there.

Also, I didn't tell him about the hiding place, or the missing money, or this email address. I promise I won't tell anyone about those things.

Terrence was concerned—asking me if I was okay, asking me if there was anything he could do. I told him I was open to suggestions, and that I was feeling a lot of different emotions at the same time, sad and confused and strangely relieved and deeply unsettled.

Because he's sweet, Terrence pretended to understand. He has some issues with his family being pretty don't-ask-don't-tell about him being gay, but I've never really let him see how monumentally messed up our family is.

We kissed goodbye, as usual. I went to my morning classes. In your honor, I didn't pay attention.

(I know that's not fair. I know you cared about some things.)

Now it's lunchtime and I'm at one of the computers in the library, making sure Mrs. Goldsmith doesn't look over my shoulder and see what I'm typing. Sloane still hasn't been found, although Joe has talked to people who've seen her at school today, so we know she isn't off somewhere with you. I think Joe's disappointed by this, but it makes sense to me, the alone part.

Poor Joe. Poor Sloane. Poor me.

You do realize how hard this is going to be, right? You do realize what you've left me with? And while I guess I'm happy you gave me the gift of plausible denial ("Really, Darren, I had no idea!"), some prep time would have been nice too.

And a goodbye. I would've liked a goodbye.

But for now, I'll settle for you telling me where you are. If you trusted me enough to give me this email, you have to trust me enough to let me know where you are, and that you're okay. If not the first part, then at least the second. You have it easy—you can picture where I am. You can imagine exactly what I'm doing. You know which computer I'm at—the same one you've found me at all year, when the library is about to close and it's time to look for another place where we can avoid home. You know what it's going to sound like when I get back and Mom and Darren yell at me some more. You know—you must know—the disappointed, heartbroken look that's going to be on Joe's face for a long time. I know you pay attention. You know things I don't know. And you also know a lot of things I *do* know. Focus on those for a minute.

I'm hoping it's not something I did. I don't want to be the reason you chose today—the reason you couldn't wait two months until you graduated. I don't think I'm the reason, but I just have to put that out there.

Lunch is almost over. I'm going to hit send. I'll be very careful to cover my tracks, to make sure no one else will find these emails. So you can write me back.

Really, Bea. Write me back. It's going to be very hard to make it through your disappearance without you.

I know you've never needed me, Bea. But fuck it—I really need you.

Write. Back.

Ezra

Subject: Me.

From: Bea <b98989898@ymail.com>

To: Ezra <e89898989@ymail.com>

Date: Tues 26 Mar 02:32 CST

Dear Ez,

I'm still breathing, if that's what you mean by okay. And no, I can't tell you where I've gone or why.

What I can tell you is that yes, I'm gone for good.

Goodbye, Hidden Valley Circle. Goodbye, Indiana.

It's surprisingly easy. When I knew I was leaving, I did a web search for "how to run away from home," and I had all the info I ever needed.

1. Only run away if you are absolutely sure. (Check.)

2. Plan ahead. (Check.)

3. Taking a friend can be helpful or harmful. (Obviously I went with harmful.)

4. Travel light. (Check.)

5. Live somewhere you can handle. (They specifically warn you against staying in a forest because "nature is cruel." Clearly whoever wrote this never lived with Mom and Darren.)
6. Leave when you won't be seen or noticed. (Check.)
7. Do not bring a cell phone or anything else that can be used to track you. (Check.)
8. Create a fake identity. (Check.)
9. Don't leave any evidence behind. (Check.)
10. Before escaping, act normal. (Check.)
11. Cut all contact and don't look back. (Check. Sort of.)

On that note, the thing about Beatrix Ahern is that running away is exactly what everyone expects of her. Sure, they'll be upset for a while, but give them a couple of months and they'll be sitting around saying, "What did you think was going to happen? There was no hope for her." Just watch. I almost wish I was going to be there to see it.

I'm sorry about the money. And I'm sorry about leaving without a goodbye. This was never meant to be a *fuck you* to you. Of all the people in my life, you're the last person I would do that to. That's why I broke the rules and created this email address. If it wasn't for you, I'd never look back.

What I can also tell you is:

I didn't leave for the reasons you're thinking.

I'm not surprised Sloane is avoiding Joe's calls.

You can feel sorry for Joe, but don't go overboard. Trust me on this.

If it ever gets too much living with Mom and Darren, go stay with Terrence. Promise.

Stop feeling guilty. The sooner you let go of that, the better.

And don't think of me as Beatrix anymore. "Beatrix" is the old life. New life, new name, or at least one I've decided to borrow for a bit. I'm not telling you this so you can try to track me down, by the way. You're my little brother and I love you, but I will always be one step ahead of you.

Love,

Me

p.s. Use a private browser every time. NEVER autofill the password. Even when you're on your own phone.

Subject: You. Missing.
From: Ezra <e89898989@ymail.com>
To: Bea <b98989898@ymail.com>
Date: Wed 27 Mar 07:45 EST

Dear BEATRIX,

I am still going to call you Bea, no matter what you end up calling yourself. Even if you want the world to see you as someone else, you'll always be Bea to me.

Also, I am not going to stop asking where you are.

I know it's not your problem anymore, but last night was not fun. Mom and Darren have gotten to the stage where they realize that having a missing daughter *does not reflect well on their parenting skills.* When I got home, the first thing they asked me wasn't if I'd seen you, but if I'd told anyone. They don't trust me either.

I was going to check if there was anything else to find in your room, but I got there a little too late, because while I was at school, Mom ransacked it. Seriously, it looked like about a hundred hounds had been unleashed to tear at everything with their teeth. I mean, it's not like your room was ever clean, but it was always messy in a really predictable way. Like how you always said you could find whatever you wanted within it—well, I kind-of could too. But not anymore. Clothes were thrown everywhere, the ones you wear all the time mixed with the ones you never wear anymore. (Which ones did you take? I haven't figured that out yet.) The stuffed animals were pulled off your bookshelf, and it looked like each one had been interrogated. Notes from Joe sat out in the open—not that many of them, and none that recent. Since he was always texting you, it was a surprise to see his handwriting. I guess he passed them to you in class, or between classes, when you weren't answering your phone.

Oh, and speaking of phones—your phone was gone.

I didn't know what to do. It was hard to be mad on your behalf, since you'd left everything in your room to fend for itself. Maybe if your room wasn't attached to the rest of the house, you would've burned it all before you left. Or maybe you don't care anymore who sees what. Which is it?

The funny thing is, even if I wasn't mad on your behalf, I was still mad. Partly, I'll admit, because I figured if they could do this to your room, there was no reason they couldn't do it to mine.

I made sure Darren was off in the den, then caught Mom in the kitchen. She had the TV on real loud but wasn't watching it. She barely looked at me when I walked in.

"What did you do to Bea's room?" I asked her.

For a moment, it was like our roles had reversed; she was the child and I was the parent who'd just caught her doing something she wasn't supposed to do. I saw her eyes admit she'd done a bad thing. But as soon as I saw it, it left.

She was leveling me with a glance now. "Don't use that voice with me. I was just trying to find her."

"Did you think she was hiding in one of her drawers? In the laundry basket?"

"Enough."

But I had to push it. "Were you looking for drugs? Did you find anything good?"

Bad move. Really bad move.

"Darren!" she called.

"Mom, come on . . ."

Darren appeared in the doorway. He was not happy to have been interrupted.

"What?" he said.

"Ezra was just telling me that Bea was *on drugs.*"

"That's not what I said!"

"Why would you ask me if I found drugs if you didn't think she was on drugs?"

I CAN'T STAND YOU! I wanted to yell. Just like ninety-nine percent of the time I'm home. How could you leave me trapped with these people? Why do I have to listen to them? I know Mom had a hard time when Dad left. I know it wasn't easy to raise us alone those few years. I am aware she is the only thing that kept us away from homelessness. I am grateful for that. But if she was smart enough to do all that, at what point did she give it up? Was it the moment she met Darren? Or was it a gradual thing? I can barely remember a time when she was on our side. I know it had to have been the case at some point. But then Darren comes along, and the lines are drawn, and we're no longer on the same side. I can barely recognize her anymore, she's so far away.

Darren's going on about how he always knew you were on drugs, how it explains the *instability*, the *irresponsibility*.

"Aren't you worried that she's hurt?" I had to ask.

"She's not hurt," Mom said flatly.

And Darren—I swear to god, Darren had to add, "No one's going to hurt your sister. She's only capable of self-inflicted wounds."

Which was amazing, coming from him. There was no point in arguing, so I didn't argue. I left.

Back in my room, I called Joe.

"What?" he answered, urgent and hopeful. "What is it?"

And I thought, yeah, he must've figured I was calling with news. Good news. But I was only calling because I didn't know who else to call. And because I wanted to see if he'd still give me a ride in the morning.

I don't need your permission to feel sorry for Joe. You have to understand—there's no way to hear the disappointment in his voice and not feel sorry for him. As for avoiding overboard—well, what's overboard in this situation, Bea? You'll have to help me out because from where I'm sitting, the person who may have gone overboard isn't Joe.

"Why isn't she calling?" he asked me.

And I told him, "Because she doesn't want us to find her."

Here's the thing: You can say things over and over to yourself, but the moment you say them out loud to someone else, they become something different, like you're taking a fear and giving it a solid shape so it can actually hurt you. And when someone else says the things you're saying in your head—that has the same effect. It should feel better to be sharing it, but it also makes it less deniable.

"She doesn't want us to find her," he repeated.

This was when I should have told him I'd heard from you. It felt selfish not to. But I also felt that if I told him, you'd know. I would have proven that you couldn't trust me.

I know you. I know I won't get a second chance. Not this time.

So instead of giving him some indication that you're alive, I asked him if he could still drive me to school in the morning. He said yes. But you can hardly be surprised by that.

Once we hung up, I called Sloane again.

She didn't answer.

I avoided dinner. Mom and Darren ate without me. When I went down later to get something from the fridge, Mom gave me a hard time. Then Darren came in, grabbed the cold pizza off my plate, threw it in the garbage, and stood in front of the fridge until I went back upstairs.

I ate some of your fruit snacks. Then I felt weird, because I know that if you don't come home, nobody else will buy them.

If I ask Mom, she'll refuse. They're yours, and if you're not here, they have no place in this house.

I know that's stupid. I know I can buy them myself. I'm just telling you how my mind is working right now.

Darren stopped by my room after I was in bed. I hate it when he does that. He always stays in the doorway, like what I have is contagious.

"Sure is quiet, isn't it?" he said.

"Yup," I said. I know better than to pretend I'm asleep. He always knows.

"Makes sense that it's quiet, without your sister blasting her music."

I did not point out that it wasn't quiet, since he kept talking. I just said, "Yup." Trying to bore him into leaving. This usually works.

"You're not like her," he said. "You're nothing like her."

I think this was meant as a compliment.

But the way he said it?

It almost sounded like an insult.

It almost sounded like he was daring me to leave.

You called it from the very start, didn't you?

When Darren came into our lives, I was ready to make him my dad. I used my crayons to draw him into our family portraits. Watched whatever show he wanted to watch. Asked him to play catch. Adored him, because that's what Mom did, and I thought I was supposed to do it too.

You saw through it, though. You resisted. Dug in. Threw tantrums on Father's Day. Refused to acknowledge his right to be at the kitchen table. I have no doubt you were the reason they got married without us there. You saw that he didn't care about us. Just her. Maybe you even knew that he'd come to convince her not to care about us either.

You fought for control of the family and lost. I just handed it over with a grin and a homemade card.

It's not like I don't think about leaving. But I also know Terrence's house is as far as I can go, realistically. After that I have nothing. No one. I mean, now I have you, out there somewhere. But right now that's nowhere I can run to. Your choice, not mine.

It was late, but I called him anyway.

"What's on your mind?" he said. He didn't ask me why I was calling. He didn't complain that I'd woken him, that it was late.

"It's so quiet here," I told him. And then I found myself saying something I don't think I've ever said before. "I'm all alone."

"No, you're not," Terrence replied.

And that was it. That was what I needed, to feel that there was someone else who remained.

I know you think I'm young. I know you think Terrence and I are both young. I don't care. I am old enough to need somebody.

I can't remember what the last words I said to you were. It's driving me crazy. I had no idea they were important.

I should send this. It's early. Mrs. Goldsmith opened the library for me when she got in. Joe wanted to find Sloane.

I wanted to find you.

Write back.

Ezra

Subject: Lunchtime.

From: Ezra <e89898989@ymail.com>

To: Bea <b98989898@ymail.com>

Date: Wed 27 Mar 12:04 EST

The email you sent yesterday said you're in another time zone. Is that why you haven't written back?

Subject: Study Hall

From: Ezra <e89898989@ymail.com>

To: Bea <b98989898@ymail.com>

Date: Wed 27 Mar 14:06 EST

It is going to drive me crazy, every time I check this inbox and find it empty. I hope you realize that.

Meanwhile, Sloane is acting weird. And I don't mean the same kind of weird as me and Joe, missing you and worried about you.

I caught her at the end of lunch, after I checked my email and saw YOU HADN'T WRITTEN BACK. (Okay, moving on.) I know Sloane's always thought of me as a pest, your over-devoted hanger-on. (I always tried to be a lovable pest. Honest. More a mouse than a rat.) But her annoyance with me always seemed like it was part of an act. This time when she saw me, I felt her want to run away. It was like she couldn't stand the sight of me.

But I guess she also knew she'd have to talk to me sooner or later. So she didn't *actually* run away.

"Do you know anything?" I asked as soon as I got to her. "Did she tell you anything?"

And do you know what she said?

She said, "She hasn't told me anything in a long time."

Then, as if she realized how harsh that was, she added, "Just leave her alone. That's the way she wants to be—absolutely alone. Fuck the rest of us. Don't make this about you. It's about her. Only her. That's also the way she wants things to be."

She was acting like she'd washed her hands of you, but I could tell you were still all over her hands. What does she know? I'm only asking because there's no way she's going to tell me. And not because she doesn't like me. Because she doesn't think I deserve to know.

I admit: I got mad. I was like, "What, you've known Bea for, what? Three years? Well, I've known her *my whole life.* She's my *sister.* I know this isn't about me. But it has something to do with me, okay? Can you at least acknowledge that?"

She just looked at me like I was as useless as an empty cereal box. Then she left.

She didn't owe me anything at all.

Also, Lisa Palmer told me her sister asked her to ask me where you are. So I guess people are figuring things out.

Help me understand this.

Ezra

Subject: Midnight

From: Ezra <e89898989@ymail.com>

To: Bea <b98989898@ymail.com>

Date: Wed 27 Mar 23:56 EST

Yes, I'm emailing you from my phone.

Your silence is cruel. You know that.

Cruel, but maybe not unusual?

Subject: RE: Midnight

From: Ezra <e89898989@ymail.com>

To: Bea <b98989898@ymail.com>

Date: Thurs 28 Mar 00:05 EST

I'm sorry. That wasn't fair.

I know this isn't about me. I know you must be dealing with things.

But still.

Subject: This is not an April Fools' Joke

From: Ezra <e89898989@ymail.com>

To: Bea <b98989898@ymail.com>

Date: Thurs 28 Mar 12:15 EST

Well, you've finally broken my streak.

For the first time ever, I've been called down to the office over the PA! That prime spot, at the end of morning announcements! "Ezra Ahern, please report to the office to see Vice Principal Southerly."

I almost didn't catch it. I thought my mind had made it up. But then I saw everyone looking at me, and Justin Ling went, "Oooooh . . . what did you do?"

I mumbled something about not knowing. You would have played it proud, badge of honor. Certified troublemaker.

The best I could do was to try not to shake when I walked into the office.

"Ezra?" the secretary said. I could see her registering what I looked like, for next time.

I nodded. She pointed me toward Mr. Southerly's office.

I headed in. He was checking something on his computer, but smiled when he saw me and gestured for me to sit down. I wasn't expecting him to be friendly, but he was.

"So," he said, "I'll get right to the point. Do you happen to know if your sister is planning to come back to school? I ask because this is the third day in a row she's missed, and when we've called your house, nobody's answered. Often this can mean a family vacation—but since you're here, and since your sister has a history of nonattendance, it felt incumbent upon me to see what was shaking."

It was so strange to have an adult talking to me rationally. Maybe that's why I answered honestly.

"I don't know for sure," I told him. "But I'd say it's not looking good for her coming back."

"Is she at home right now? Do you think I'd be able to talk to her?"

"No, sir," I said. "I don't think that's possible."

I could feel how mad Mom and Darren would be at me for saying this. But it's not like they gave me another answer to offer.

Mr. Southerly looked me in the eye, and it wasn't threatening at all. If anything, I had a sense he had at least an inkling of what I was feeling.

"Look," he said, "Beatrix is eighteen, so there isn't anything I can do. And I'm not going to put you in the position of go-between. I just want you to know I'm concerned, and that I'm here for both of you. I know at her age, school can feel unimportant, and graduation can seem unimportant. But that impulse never serves your future well. You don't have to tell me where she is . . . but do you know if she's safe?"

"I think so."

"And has there been trouble at home?"

Here's where my honesty failed me. I couldn't say *There's always trouble at home.* Because that's just an invitation for further questions. Further trouble.

The weird thing is: I felt like Mr. Southerly already knew the real answer. Maybe you made more of an impression than you thought. Or maybe he's just seen this situation plenty of times before. Maybe there's nothing at all original about us and our family, Bea. Isn't that sad?

"There hasn't been anything out of the ordinary," I told him.

He nodded. Also registering me.

"Well," he said, standing up from his desk, "know that I'm here. I'll keep trying to contact your parents. I won't tell them we had this talk—what's said in this office stays in this office. Come back anytime. Understood?"

Now it was my turn to nod, even though all I wanted to do was disappear.

I can't spend my whole lunch writing to you. I need to do something else. And you need to write back to me.

Ezra

Subject: Sorry

From: Bea <b989898989@ymail.com>

To: Ezra <e89898989@ymail.com>

Date: Thurs 28 Mar 03:09 CST

Ezra,

If I could make you understand, don't you know I would?

Me

Subject: more

From: Bea <b98989898@ymail.com>

To: Ezra <e89898989@ymail.com>

Date: Thurs 28 Mar 03:26 CST

Ez,

I should never have given you this email address. You always do this. I can't do all I need to do *and* worry about you. I've never been good at doing two things at once, you know that.

I don't think you have a clue what it's like to let everybody down all the time. In fact, I know you don't know what it's like, good little overachiever that you are. I'm not surprised Mom and Darren don't sound more upset, but it might be nice to hear *some* concern for, I don't know, my *safety and well-being*.

For instance, not to go too far back into the archives, but do you remember when I was eleven and fell off my bike and walked around *all day* with a broken arm until they came home from work and decided to take me to the doctor—only after they'd made sure I wasn't bluffing? As if I'd ever made things like that up, because I learned in the wee early hours of my life that pretending you were sick or injured wasn't a way to get attention.

But the truth is I haven't been okay in a long time. Maybe

never. You see, here's something no one knows—I worry. At night, when everyone else was sleeping, I would just lie there and think about every bad thing that could happen to me or you. I would think about Joe's accident and how he almost died and what that would have meant for me, being alone in this world without him, and how he might be the last boy who would ever love me. I would think about Sloane and what would happen if we stopped being friends. I would worry that something would break Joe and me up. That something would make Sloane stop talking to me or turn on me like so many girls do to each other. I would worry that Mom would get in an accident and die and leave us alone with Darren, or that you and Terrence would break up and you would be lost and sad, or that Darren would murder us all in our sleep, and I would worry that somehow all of it would be my fault.

Most of all, I worried about you. That Darren would hurt you or Mom would hurt you and I wouldn't be able to get in between you fast enough. That I'm not enough to protect you and keep you safe. That something would happen to you and I wouldn't be there to stop it.

I even worried about Dad. That's how bad it got.

So you see, I care more than you think. About *everything*.

Maybe I got tired of letting people down. Of everyone expecting me to be someone who would do something exactly like this—just disappear. No matter how many A's I got in school, no matter how many grades ahead I was reading. Not even when

I tutored that girl, Celia What's-her-name, during recess because my teacher asked me to, and I did it every single day for two months, even when Celia threatened to kill me if I actually taught her anything. Maybe there's a part of me that was like, why not do it then? Just give them what they expect? But that's not why I left.

The trouble with worrying so much is that sometimes you worry something into coming true.

Maybe I just needed to be someone who does the opposite of worry.

But that's all I can tell you. Don't ask me for more because I won't/can't give it to you.

This is going to be the last you hear from me for a while. I know it's no use saying this, but please don't take it personally. It's not personal. This isn't about you or Joe (directly, at least) or Sloane (even though she'd like to think so) or dear, blind Mr. Southerly or even Darren and Mom. This is about me.

Take care of yourself. I love you. If you write, I won't get it. Or maybe I will get it, but I won't read it. I can't. Not right now.

Love,
Me

p.s. Lisa Palmer and her sister can kiss my ass.

Subject: p.s.

From: Bea <b98989898@ymail.com>

To: Ezra <e89898989@ymail.com>

Date: Fri 29 Mar 09:11 CST

So I didn't sleep last night (surprise) because I felt bad about the email. And then I started worrying about leaving you. I'm just angry, Ez. Really angry. Sorry if that came out at you.

p.s. Lisa Palmer and her sister can still kiss my ass.

Subject: ARE YOU OK?

From: Bea <b989898898@ymail.com>

To: Ezra <e89898989@ymail.com>

Date: Fri 5 Apr 12:32 CST

Ez,

I know I told you not to contact me, but let's face it, I didn't really expect you to listen to me. I'm on email for the first time in days, and there's nothing from you. Are you trying to get back at me? Teach me a lesson? We've been through too much for this silent treatment bullshit.

Me

Subject: ARE YOU OK?

From: Bea <b98989898@ymail.com>

To: Ezra <e89898989@ymail.com>

Date: Sat 6 Apr 06:43 CST

Where are you?

Subject: EZ! ARE YOU OK?

From: Bea <b98989898@ymail.com>

To: Ezra <e89898989@ymail.com>

Date: Sun 7 Apr 18:01 CST

I'm sorry!

Subject: Seriously. ARE YOU OK? NO REALLY, ARE YOU ALIVE?

From: Bea <b98989898@ymail.com>

To: Ezra <e89898989@ymail.com>

Date: Mon 8 Apr 07:10 CST

Remember when Joe had his accident? Remember how before we knew he'd had an accident I got this cold-all-over feeling and almost passed out? That same thing just happened to me. If you're screwing with me, I'm going to be so, so mad at you.

Subject: HELLO?!?!?!?!?!?!?!

From: Bea <b98989898@ymail.com>

To: Ezra <e89898989@ymail.com>

Date: Tues 9 Apr 14:22 CST

I know how you hate it when people write all in caps, but THIS ISN'T FUNNY, LITTLE BROTHER! WHERE ARE YOU? I promise I won't disappear completely, not from you. If you email me, I'll email back. Just. Please. Email. Me. Already. I left you this email, Ez, the least you could do is use it.

Your concerned big sister who is REALLY TRYING NOT TO FREAK THE HELL OUT,

Bea

Subject: Help

From: Bea <b98989898@ymail.com>

To: Ezra <e89898989@ymail.com>

Date: Wed 10 Apr 21:01 CST

Holy shit, Ez.

I heard about what happened. It was on the news, Ez! The fucking news! I'm barely gone five minutes. WTF?

I need you to get on a bus, train, helicopter, whatever, and meet me at Union Station in St. Louis (that's in Missouri). Outside the planetarium.

Remember the list of rules for running away. DO EVERYTHING IT SAYS.

Kiss Terrence goodbye. Tell him you love him. Tell him everything you want him to hear in case this is your last conversation, except that you're leaving. That's the thing you can't say.

I'll be waiting. Let me know you got this. As soon as you know when you're coming in, tell me. After that, this email will destruct in five, four, three, two . . .

Love,

B

p.s. Do not bring your phone!

Subject: The News

From: Ezra <e89898989@ymail.com>

To: Bea <b98989898@ymail.com>

Date: Thurs 11 Apr 04:19 EST

So there is something considerably fucked up about desperately worrying about someone and then having her say that she's through with worrying, like you can just flick a switch and, wow, all the worrying is gone, only you're still there and your switch must be stuck because you keep worrying and worrying and she says, sorry, I can't really talk right now, and have a nice life, because my life is clearly much, much more important than yours, so sorry, sucks to be you. And, okay, you think—she's handing you scissors and holding the cord real tight so all it will take is one quick snip, so you should cut it, JUST CUT IT, and that way whenever you're in school and everyone's looking at you weird and whenever you're at home and everyone's looking at you weird, you can just hold up your end of it and say, sorry, no cord, no connection, no way of contacting her, so don't worry—oh, wait, Bea . . . you're not worrying. *I'm* the only one worrying, because I can't seem to stop. Stupid *stupid* me. I thought I was the exception, I thought I was worth holding on to—but nope. When someone tells you that, what do you do? Well, you listen to her,

And the missing girl's best friend is as forthcoming as a fucking mime, which the boyfriend takes to mean she has something to hide. (An understandable reaction, no?) So boyfriend's gone from sad to pissed. Best friend is one of those see-no-evil, hear-no-evil monkeys. And the missing girl is like *see ya.* So who can the brother confide in? His mother! Surely, his mother has *some* maternal instinct left. Surely, there's got to be an ounce of maternal instinct in there somewhere! It's been a week since he's really talked to anyone and she catches him one night at a really vulnerable moment and he says to her, "This really sucks, doesn't it?" And do you know what she says? She says, "It's probably for the best." And he knows he should keep his mouth shut. **HE KNOWS THIS.** But he can't help it. He looks at his mother and says, "Who the fuck are you?" And she slaps him. Yells for her husband, screams to him what's happened, works in the word *ungrateful* (as she often does), and then the husband pauses to make it clear what's about to happen, that three-second pause where he decides exactly how he's going to beat the shit out of you. This time, it's the shove-against-the-wall, punch-in-the-gut one-two. You can see that, right? You can see exactly how that would play out, no? Hubby says, "Don't talk that way to your mother!" and I'm actually thinking, *If I fire her from being my mother, does that mean I can talk to her any way I want? And you?* Like, I just want to quit the whole family. Even you, although as he's yelling at me and decking me I'm certainly understanding at least part of why you're not here. I just start howling. There's no other word

Carson and Walter are also in the car, and I can see they're not entirely understanding why Joe's bothering to pick me up. They also don't understand why I'm holding a purse. I tell them I was left holding the bag, har har, and Joe's the only one who laughs. (Strangely, nobody comments on the fact that I'm beaten up. Or maybe that's not strange at all.) When we get to the movie theater, I leave the purse in the car, under the front seat. But I take the wallet in with me, and use the ATM as much as I can. (Mom's password is Darren's birthday. Awwwwwww.) I go into the movie and sit with the guys, last one in. Right during the previews, my phone starts buzzing like crazy. It won't stop. I look and see it's Darren calling. And—I know, stupid—my rage answers the phone and says, "Can't talk—I'm in a movie," then hangs up. Hysterical, right? I turn off my phone. It isn't twenty minutes later when I feel my arm yanked out of its socket and, look, it's Darren in the aisle, and he's hollering at me in the middle of the movie. Completely drunk on his own rage—no alcohol needed! People are shushing him and he's breaking my arm, so I try to pull away and that's when he really starts going to town and other people start screaming because—hey!—Darren's brought his gun, and guns are a big no-no in crowded movie theaters nowadays. Carson and Walter are peeing themselves from fear, but Joe's on his feet and saying, "Sir!" to Darren, like he's going to talk Darren down, and that's when the movie theater security guard comes storming in and draws *his* gun. Someone has the wisdom to stop the movie and turn on the lights—people are shrieking and they're all pushing to get out of there, and Darren may be a mean bastard but he has no desire to be shot, so he puts his gun down and says that—swear to God!—*this is a private matter between him and his son,* and I'm like, "I am NOT your son," which confuses things even more, and we all just hold there—Carson and Walter leave, but Joe stays—until the police come and Darren is taken away. And, yeah, it makes the news—but, you know what, I don't think it makes the St. Louis news. I think this means you were online checking out the news from back home. I'm not sure if they mentioned the house—Joe drove by later and it's still there, so my damage was likely limited to the kitchen. The news stations probably focused on Darren, with interviews of people who were trapped in the theater saying how scared they were that it was another shooting. But I'm going to be honest with you—I wasn't scared. I was *pissed.* At him. At Mom. At you. At everyone, including myself. I was *supremely* pissed at myself. Because now there's no going back. And I'll be honest—part of me would've liked to leave the bridge up instead of burning it. I'm not sure if you feel the same—I guess time will tell. Oh, and by the way, I'm not going to Union Station in St. Louis. I am not getting rid of my phone, because you know what? It's one of the only things I have left.

This is how my new life begins: on the top bunk where Joe's brother Max used to sleep before he headed off to that party school and never looked back. With Darren in jail, or maybe not in jail. For a while, Terrence texted every five minutes, asking if I was okay, and I answered every six minutes, saying yeah. Because how could I even begin to explain it? Now he's asleep and Joe's asleep and you're asleep in some room I can't picture, maybe with someone I can't picture. It's really late and I'm not even sure what else to say to you. You know now that I'm not coming. But here's the thing: The cord hasn't been cut. The bridge between us hasn't burned because who the fuck builds bridges out of flammable materials? We spent way too much time putting those stones in place, sister of mine. You are getting another chance to be truthful with me. And I mean *really* truthful. I believe you when you say you were worried about things. But I don't believe you when you make it seem like that's the only reason you left. If we're going to do this—if we're going to start new lives—we have to do it right. Believe me, there's a part of me that wants to go to you, that wants to ride passenger seat on whatever journey you're on. But I'm not sure that's what I should do. Because you're right—you've never been good at doing two things at once, and if there's something you need to do, supporting me isn't going to make it any easier. And if I go to you and you fuck it up—I will never get over that. So you do you, and I'll do here. There's also the fact that I can't just leave school. I can't just leave Terrence. I can't just leave everything I've ever known. I've left Mom and Darren. Irrevocably. But I'm not ready to leave here, especially because you haven't told me a single thing about where I'd be going and what I'd be doing there.

I started this email much angrier at you than I am now. I really wish you'd been there to see the look on Darren's face when the police showed up, when it dawned on him what kind of shit he was in. (Oh, and my arm wasn't broken . . . just bruised. I think the cops were focused so much on getting him out of there that they didn't really focus on me. And Joe and I didn't exactly stick around to talk to them. There were plenty of other people willing to be witnesses.)

It's time to tell me what you're doing, what your life is like now. Even if you don't want to tell me why you left . . . I will give you (for now) a pass on talking about the past as long as you tell me about the present. I'm not going to tell anyone—you should know that by now. And I'm not going to show up there—you should know that too. But if we're going to have new lives, let's at least tell each other about them. And if it gets worse here, I know what station to head toward.

I didn't do any of this to make you worry. It wasn't about you—and while your departure may have been an indirect cause of the events that led to the Showdown at the Regal, it feels like it would have happened anyway, even if you'd stayed. The rage on both sides was waiting to be triggered. I'm not telling you all of this to make you worry more. If anything, you should worry a little less about me. I'm out of there. I am going to figure this out.

Meanwhile, school is going to be verrrrrry interesting tomorrow . . . and by tomorrow, I mean in three hours.

Your (newly liberated OR woefully screwed) brother,
Ezra

Subject: Holy Shit, Ez.

From: Bea <b98989898@ymail.com>

To: Ezra <e89898989@ymail.com>

Date: Thurs 11 Apr 11:34 CST

Oh, Ez. My life isn't more important than yours. Don't you see? For so long, I thought my life was the least important thing.

If I'm being fair, I can't blame that completely on Mom and Darren. (Well, maybe Darren.) She had her moments, right? I'm not misremembering that? Like when I got my period for the first time and bled all over my jeans, and Darren had a fit because we weren't "made of money" (as if I'd done it on purpose), and Mom took me into the bathroom and told me he was just a man, he couldn't understand. "You let me handle Darren," she said, and then she went to the grocery store and bought my favorite cake—that Raspberry Dream cake, which was like eighty percent frosting, the one I only had on birthdays.

There was also a trip we took, just you, me, Mom. This was BD, Before Darren, and for five happy days it was the three of us, and we got in the car and drove to the beach. Somewhere in the Carolinas. I remember white sand and grassy dunes and picking up sand dollars. Mom bleached them white for us, and at night we crawled into her bed and I read *Coraline* aloud until we fell asleep, one by one, and before we left she told us she loved us and to never forget it.

I'm not making that up, am I? If I am, don't tell me.

But even then, even in the best moments, I never felt my life was *important.* To you and me, maybe. But not to anyone else. Not even to Mom, not even when it was just Mom and me, before you, before Darren. Because the thing I always knew is that somehow I was in her way. Not just because she told me so once. But because I felt it.

Do you know how many times I've wanted to do what you did? Just light a match. *Poof.* Goodbye, Mom. Goodbye, Darren. Goodbye, house.

I guess, in a way, that was what I did by leaving. I guess, in a way, that's what we've both done.

Subject: My New Life

From: Bea <b98989898@ymail.com>

To: Ezra <e89898989@ymail.com>

Date: Thurs 11 Apr 11:46 CST

My first night here, I slept on the grounds of the St. Louis Art Museum, which is in this area called the Hill. It made me feel safer somehow being near all that priceless art, like, with all that stupidly expensive security, nothing could happen to me as long as I remained on the grounds. Not that I'm a priceless piece of art, but I'm the only me I have. During the day, I've been walking a lot, trying to learn the city. I've decided I like the Hill neighborhood best. It's filled with Italian markets and Italian restaurants and Catholic churches flying the Italian flag and one- and two-story houses with tidy yards. The air here smells like Mario's Good Family Food—warm and rich and full of spices—only even more mouth-watering. (Remember the time we sneaked into their kitchen and stole an entire vat of breadsticks and hid them in our garage? And lived on them for *two weeks straight* and Mom never caught on?) (Insert evil laugh here.) I found a hostel on the Hill, but it's $30 a night and crowded, and you know I don't sleep well around other people. Not Sloane. Not even Joe. You're the only one, Ez. When you were little and convinced that Bigfoot lived in your closet, I would lie on the floor by your bed and stay awake as long as I could just to make sure you felt safe. But at some point, always, I would drift off. Those are the only times I ever remember having good dreams, sleeping there on your floor. Because I felt like I was doing something good and unselfish, like somehow I'd found my calling—to keep the monsters away from my little brother. I wish I'd been better at it.

Anyway. If I need to, I can go back to the art museum, which is free and quiet and has a night sky with more stars than I know what to do with. So I'm okay. It's you I'm worried about.

Subject: More.

From: Bea <b98989898@ymail.com>

To: Ezra <e89898989@ymail.com>

Date: Thurs 11 Apr 12:31 CST

What My Life Is Like Now

There is loneliness. And guilt. And worry over what I've done to you. There is fear about what comes next and what will I do and will I have to go back home—a home with no you—tail between my legs, and beg the forgiveness of Mom and Darren and be a good girl forever and ever amen. There is this big fat nagging doubt in the very back of my mind that says: YOU CAN'T DO THIS. YOU WILL FAIL. YOU WILL ALWAYS FAIL AT EVERYTHING, NO MATTER WHAT YOU DO, BECAUSE THAT IS WHO YOU ARE. YOU ARE A LOSER. YOU ARE A FAILURE. YOU ARE NOTHING.

I try not to listen to it, but when someone tells you those things enough, you can't help it. Because if they speak loud enough and often enough, that's the only voice you're able to hear. I try to remind myself it's not *my* doubt, it's the doubt of *them.* Namely Darren, who put it there. Did I doubt myself before he came along? Before Mom fell under his spell and forgot every single maternal instinct she ever had? I can't remember because it's been going on for so long. Can you remember? Like, did we ever believe in ourselves, really believe in ourselves? Maybe it's not fair to lump you into that, so let me rephrase: Did I ever really believe in myself without stopping to worry or play devil's advocate or think, *You can't do that, Bea. You're not smart enough, brave enough, nice enough, pretty enough, funny enough, enough-enough.*

Now when the fat, nagging doubt gets too loud in my brain, I say, GO AWAY, DOUBT. GO AWAY OR I WILL SET YOU ON FIRE BECAUSE APPARENTLY SETTING THINGS ON FIRE IS SOMETHING THAT RUNS IN THIS FAMILY, AND I WILL BURN YOU DOWN TO THE GROUND LIKE A HOUSE.

And I stop listening to anyone but me.

Because here's the other thing about my life now: I'm free.

Free.

In case you don't recognize the word, it means this: I can be anything. Anyone. Sometimes I'm Bea. Sometimes I'm Veronica. Or Kelsey. Or Claire. Or Pippa. Or No One At All. I'm free to fuck up without someone holding it over my head or saying, *That's just Bea, she always fucks things up.* Without someone saying, *See there? See what you did? That's what you always do. Why should we ever expect anything out of someone like you when you only let everybody down?* I can screw everything up out here, with no one to see but me, and you know what? The world doesn't end. It keeps right on going and so do I.

I'm also free to get things right and to actually do some good without anyone making a big deal over it because it's *just so out of character and unexpected.* I'm free to do whatever, whenever, and there's no one here to judge me or tell me I can't, I shouldn't, I won't, I'd better not or else. I'm scared shitless. But I'm also braver than I ever knew.

Here's another thing. I can sleep during the day and stay up all night. You know how I love night. The darkness. The stars. Houses all lit up inside. Everything is clean and quiet and peaceful in the dark. You can't see all the dirt and the trash and the scars everywhere, on everything, on everybody. So many scars. Night is clean. Night is safe. So I stay awake and pretend this is what the world looks like all the time.

And here's another thing. I'm smart. Okay, I always knew this, but there's *I'm too smart to study because school bores me* smart and there's *I'm surviving one day at a time out in the big, bad world because of me and no one else, and I'm still here and no one's hurt me yet because I will never let anyone hurt me again* smart. Well, guess what? I'm both kinds, only I never would have known I was the second one because, according to the people back home (pretty much everyone but you), I'm A LOSER, A FAILURE, A NOTHING.

It's amazing what you can learn about yourself when you get away from the doubters. (And that includes Sloane, but maybe not Joe. Poor Joe, who will always feel the way other people tell him to feel and will never actually think or feel for himself.)

Here's one last thing because I've already given you enough. As you can probably tell, I still don't want to be found, so as soon as I finish writing this email I'll go back over it a few dozen times and make sure I haven't said too much.

But I owe you this.

So here it is.

In this new life, this one I'm chasing, I have a chance to be loved. Me. Unlovable, unlikable, terrible me. Belligerent Bea. Difficult Bea. Bad Seed Bea.

Imagine it.

Not the kind of love Mom gave us, which was barely love at all. And not the kind of love I had with Joe. I was with Joe because he was expected and he was sweet and he was boring and he was safe in a way I'd never known safe. And then he had the accident, and I was nice to him because how could I not be? You're kind of forced to be nice after someone is in *an accident.* I couldn't break up with him, not then, not after that. I didn't have a choice. Unless I just stopped being there altogether.

I don't feel bad about Mom but I do feel bad about Joe. Not bad enough to stay, obviously, but bad.

This person who shall remain nameless (for now) is a lot like me, but he's also better than me in every way. And he makes me feel like I can do anything.

He almost silences the doubt. Almost.

He is funny and also serious.

And smart—smarter than me, maybe even smarter than you.

He's weird too—weirder than me, maybe even weirder than you. Like he's superstitious about black cats and 11:11 and not making left-hand turns. He will drive for miles out of his way just to get where he needs to go. And he never picks up pennies for luck because he leaves them for other people, and if he sees a penny tail-side up, he flips it over so it's lucky. Which is lovely, and also weird.

But he knows that he's weird and I'm weird and everyone is weird, deep down, even if they pretend they're not, and that's okay. He doesn't want to change me.

He makes me feel *possible.*

Remember when Sloane and I were reading *The Metamorphosis* for old Mrs. Nadel's class? That book Kafka wrote about the salesman who woke up one day *as an insect*? And he stays shut up in his room and becomes this huge burden to his family (because, hello, he's a GIANT BUG!), and his little sister has to go to work to help support them, and they all just wish he was dead? And then he DOES die, and they're all so thankful and relieved because WHO WANTS AN INSECT FOR A SON?

Well, that's how I was feeling back home—like Gregor Samsa, the giant, monstrous bug that no one wanted. But now, out here, away from it all, it's like I've transformed into the Me I'm meant to be.

A Me who apparently likes to write Ezra-length letters, but at least you know why I've run away. Only I like to think it's not so much running away as running *to,* even though there is A LOT to run away from (and I don't just mean Mom and Darren). I am running toward life and freedom and me.

What I wish for you, Ez, more than anything, is all those same things. Life and freedom and your own metamorphosis into *you.* You say you're liberated now. But are you?

Write me back and let me know how school is. I promise to read it. I promise to respond. Because you are worth holding on to, and I may have quit everyone else, but I'm not quitting you. Even when I didn't believe in myself, I believed in you. My only regret in leaving is not dragging you with me.

Love,
Your sister, Gregor Samsa

p.s. I guess I owe Joe a thank-you for taking in my baby brother. If you can't be here or with Terrence, I'd much rather you be there than at home. Just do me a favor and be careful.

Subject: What? Who?

From: Ezra <e89898989@ymail.com>

To: Bea <b98989898@ymail.com>

Date: Thurs 11 Apr 13:48 EST

You know how you figure something is going to be surreal—maybe not *Metamorphosis* surreal, but real-life surreal—and then when you're actually at the moment you've been dreading, it's about a hundred times weirder than you imagined it would be?

Well, that's today at school. I'm like a celebrity, but in that high school way that a kleptomaniac or a murder victim is a celebrity. Only I'm not a criminal and I'm still alive. For the past week, it's felt like anyone who saw me was seeing me as your brother. Now they're seeing me as me, or maybe as that insane-potential-movie-theater-shooter's son.

And as all this is going on, do you know what I keep thinking about?

Your guy. Your mystery man.

Frankly?

What. The. Fuck?

I don't understand anything. I mean, how can you be free if you're following someone?

Shit. People are coming over.

Subject: Who? What?

From: Ezra <e89898989@ymail.com>

To: Bea <b98989898@ymail.com>

Date: Fri 12 Apr 01:34 EST

I think Joe is starting to suspect that I'm lying to him.

I'm in his backyard right now. I kept waiting for him to go to sleep, but he wouldn't go to sleep. So finally I said I was going to step outside to chat with Terrence. And Joe was like, "Why can't you chat with Terrence in here?" And all I could think to say was "It's *private,*" which made me sound like a ten-year-old with a bogus secret, and also made me sound pretty ungrateful, because Joe's stepped up for me even though there isn't much reason for him to do so. There's something I've noticed, though—whenever my phone lights up with a message, he looks at the screen. Wanting to see who it is. So I've tried to keep my phone in my pocket.

Anyway, he's upstairs now, thinking who knows what. I'm worried he'll ask Terrence about it tomorrow—*Why did you have to chat with Ezra so late? What couldn't wait six hours until you saw him in school?* Terrence will cover for me, but he'll also call me on it. I have no idea what I'll tell him.

Don't take this the wrong way, but how do you manage to lie

to so many people at once? How can you do that without starting to feel like all you are is a lie?

I still need to tell you about school. You know who was coming up to me at lunch? Jessica Wei. Remember Jessica? She and I were friends in elementary school. And we've been friendly-but-not-really-friends ever since. She headed over to me with those girls who follow her everywhere, Serena and Taz, and she came right out and asked me what happened last night. And it was weird, because I could tell she wasn't doing it to be gossipy, like your favorite, Lisa Palmer. But it wasn't like she was concerned either. Like, she wasn't asking me if I was okay. She was asking the question because she wanted to know the answer . . . and I was the only person around who could give it to her.

I felt all the usual rules trying to block out the answer. No, not rules. Commandments. *If anything goes wrong at home, you can't tell anyone outside of home. Pity is worse than pain, embarrassment is worse than help. If people treat you like shit, you still have to stay loyal to them. You still have to give them the benefit of the doubt that maybe you are, in fact, shit and deserve to be treated the way they treat you.*

You know what I mean.

We might not have been turned into bugs, but we were always made aware of how easily we could be stepped on.

But not anymore. That's what I decided then, as the commandments started to blare. Not. Anymore.

So I told Jessica, “My stepfather is an asshole and he found a way to register this fact with the entire world.”

I looked at Serena and said, “The only surprise was that usually when he wants to vent his rage, he thinks he’s enough of a weapon himself that he doesn’t need a gun.”

I turned to Taz and wrapped it up with, “In fairness to him, I had just tried to burn his house down. But in fairness to me, he deserved worse.”

I thought they’d run away. I thought they’d laugh. I thought they’d pull out their phones and ask me to say it again so they could send it to their friends.

I didn’t care.

But you know what came next? Before I knew what was happening, Jessica was hugging me. Not saying a word. Just holding me tight, as Serena and Taz, who I barely know, looked on approvingly. Then, when she pulled back, Jessica said, “It’s going to be okay.” Which isn’t true, but is something people say when they want it to be okay.

Do you think she already knew about the fucked-up state of our family? Do you think other people know? I thought we faked it so well. Mom talked to the ladies at the supermarket like her life was endless coupons and free desserts. Darren came to my soccer games and cheered. The other dads liked him. What did Jessica Wei see?

We thought there was a wall around our story. But what if there were windows?

What could I say to Jessica, at the moment she actually cared? I said I was okay. I said I'd found somewhere else to stay.

She told me they were heading to lunch. She asked if I wanted to sit with them.

I nearly lost it. Bea, this is so weird. I don't know how to be this kind of visible.

I said thanks, but I'd already had lunch. (Lie.) It felt monumental enough to tell them something. I wasn't ready to have a conversation.

They left. I could have written you more, but instead I tracked down Terrence. I told him I had to talk to him, I had to tell him things . . . and then, after school, we went to the woods and I said I needed to go to the house and see if Mom and Darren were there, and if they weren't there, I needed to get some things. I told him I couldn't do it alone.

You know how I feel about Terrence. You know how sweet he is, to a degree that's sometimes annoying and sometimes deeply intimidating. You know I didn't think we'd last two weeks, and now we've lasted seven months. He's been there for me—but this is something different. He's been there for me, but I've never *asked* for him to be there. I've never admitted—except on a superficial, social level—that I've needed him there.

He agreed to go with me. Of course he agreed to go with me. And along the way, I told him what happened last night. I did a Q&A with myself, because I knew he wouldn't ask me questions with the same ferocity that I would. I spun them backwards, and the answers got harder the closer we got to the source.

What happened at the movie theater? I asked.

I told him.

How did you get there?

I told him.

Why were you running from your house?

I told him.

Why did you set the paper towels on fire?

Why did you run to the kitchen?

Why did your mother hit you?

Why did you say that to your mother?

I told him.

Why doesn't your mother love you?

This is when it got weird, because I didn't know why I asked myself that, and I didn't know what my answer would be until I said it.

"She does love me. She just doesn't love me enough."

Is that why Bea left?

"No. It's probably part of it. But no, I don't think so."

We were a few houses away from our house. The whole time I was talking in reverse, I was following my footsteps in reverse. I didn't even realize until I was there.

"I'll go check," Terrence said.

I nodded.

Then I tried to hide, just in case Mom or Darren drove by. (For all I know, Darren is still in jail. But that's not something I could count on.) I felt like a burglar in my own neighborhood. Terrence came back in a few minutes and told me Mom's car was there. He thought he'd seen her in the kitchen window.

I abandoned the plan. I don't want to see her. Even if that bastard's still in jail.

Terrence didn't argue. We went back to his house. His parents weren't home—his dad still at work, his mom off at a Black Women's Action Group meeting. Normally an empty house would be an invitation for some quality cuddling. But when we curled up together in his room, it felt different. When we cuddled before, it was the cuddling of certainty, of knowing we were meant to be together, and proving it as much as we could. But this? It was the cuddling of uncertainty. My uncertainty. He asked me some things—how long am I going to stay at Joe's? Do I want him to talk to his parents about staying with him? And I answered. But mostly we drifted off into our own thoughts, largely unshareable.

I ate dinner there, after his parents got home. They didn't say anything about Darren, leading me to believe that they are either spectacularly polite or completely oblivious to what goes on in our town. (Of course, Terrence's father still thinks of me as Terrence's "special friend," so obliviousness isn't *that* shocking.)

Then I came back to Joe's. We played some video games. We

didn't talk. He just looked at my phone every time I got a message, and didn't think I saw him do it.

Now I'm here in the backyard. It's long past midnight on a school night—think I'll get grounded?

I know I should go to bed. But there's one question I have to answer before I do that.

You asked if we ever believed in ourselves. And, Bea . . . I think the answer's yes. But the weird thing? I think we believed in ourselves most when we were pretending to be other people. Iron Man and Black Widow. Han Solo and Chewbacca. We were great pretenders—defenders of the backyard, guardians of the rec-room peace. When we stepped out of our own story and into others, we would be these laughing, excited, fearless kids. Maybe I saw it this way because I was the younger one. Maybe you were humoring me. I don't know if this counts, and I don't know if it's real. But when you and I were pretending to save the world, I actually believed we were capable of saving the world.

We had that. We didn't have much else, except each other. But we had that.

Write more soon,
Ezra

Subject: The Great Pretenders

From: Bea <b98989898@ymail.com>

To: Ezra <e89898989@ymail.com>

Date: Sat 13 Apr 18:52 CST

Dear Ez,

So how does it feel to be popular?

Or should I say notorious?

Either way, I'm glad people are behaving themselves for now.

Do you remember when Jessica Wei missed school for like an entire month a couple of years ago? It's because her brother broke her jaw. (I think she blamed it on gymnastics, but it wasn't gymnastics. He. Broke. Her. Jaw.) They had to put him in a home somewhere because they were scared of him. That's the rumor at least. So she has that special X-ray vision that allows her to spot another person who's been pushed around, no matter how they're trying to hide it. (And we were good at hiding it. We had to be.)

Joe is a nosy one. I know he's concerned and he misses me, and blah blah blah. I don't mean that to sound heartless, but he was always nosy, even when I was right there. He couldn't just let you be. He had to know *everything*. And he was *everywhere*. He wanted to do everything together, and maybe that's nice at the start, but after a while I couldn't breathe. It was like this really warm, comfy blanket that felt good at first, but then the blanket wants to wrap itself tighter and tighter around your body, and not just your body, but your neck and your head and your whole fucking face, and that blanket just clamps right onto you and holds on like it's trying to be a second skin, and before you know it you feel like you're going to just drop dead from all that holding and not being able to breathe. That's the kind of nosy he is.

Terrence, on the other hand, is a good egg. I know he bugs you sometimes, but honestly, he's good, decent people, and we both know that's hard to find. Let him in a little. You can tell him you've heard from me, that you still hear from me, but that's it, nothing more. Then make him swear on his life that he won't say a word to anyone.

How do you lie to so many people at once? You do it because you don't have a choice and because it's all you know and because all you've done is lie your whole entire life. We became liars the minute Darren arrived. Actually before that. We became liars when Dad left, although I was too young to remember it and you weren't even born. The second he disappeared, Mom started telling us he didn't want us anymore. And the only thing we could do was believe her, and later on we told everyone he was killed in a fire (ironically enough), trying to save a family of five. Why a fire? I don't know. Why a family of five? Because we thought that sounded nice. A mom, a dad, three kids. Everything normal

Subject: A Day in the Life of Bea

From: Bea <b98989898@ymail.com>

To: Ezra <e89898989@ymail.com>

Date: Sun 14 Apr 11:47 CST

I walk to the market at the end of the street. It's an Italian market, of course, being located on the Hill, and it smells like sweet vinegar and garlic. There is a man who works behind the long wooden counter who looks like he's been there since they opened, back in 1923. His name is Franco, and he has the bushiest eyebrows I've ever seen. The first time I go in, he watches me like a hawk. I have to pick up every single bottle and jar and vegetable because it's all beautiful, like instruments from some foreign world. All I can think is *People cook with these things. People come here and put this in their basket and then they take it home to their nice house, with their nice family, and they cook a delicious meal instead of ordering pizza or throwing down a cereal box and shouting, "Dinner's ready."*

All this careful examination makes old Franco antsy, like he's afraid I'm going to steal something, but instead of following me around the store or yelling at me, he says, "Kid, I'll make you a deal. You don't steal from me, and I won't steal from you." I think, *The joke's on you, buddy, because I've got nothing you'd ever want to steal.* But instead I say, "Deal."

So now I go in there every day. It's the only routine I have in this new life. Franco's wife, Irene, is the one who buys everything for the shop. She has long gray-black hair that she piles on her head, and a vast collection of parrot earrings. She says one of their daughters lives in San Diego and is always sending them to her even though Irene hates birds. All I hear is what a good mom she is, wearing these earrings she doesn't like just because her daughter sends them to her.

Yesterday, Franco let me use the computer in his office. Before that, it was the public library, but today I'm sitting here in this big wooden chair with wheels, an ancient metal fan creaking out air at me. There's a big daybed with lots of pillows and a red blanket and posters of Italy framed on the walls. (Irene reads interior design books when she isn't shopping for the store.) The office smells like spices and I'm hopeful. Not happy. Not yet. But hopeful. When was the last time you could say that?

You'd love the library, by the way. I know reading's always been more my thing, but you have to see this place, Ez. Marble floors, arched windows, ceilings as high as the treetops, chandeliers straight out of Hogwarts. Sometimes I go there in the mornings, choose a stack of books, and read until they close.

Back to Franco's.

Right now, right this minute as I type these words, I'm sitting here breathing. This is one of the things I do in my new life. I breathe. Today I'm not looking over my shoulder, afraid Mom and Darren will walk in, because there's only the one door, leading to the market, and the longer I'm away from them, the easier I feel. The easier I breathe.

The art museum isn't far from here, but far enough so it's not right next door. Same with the hostel. Just in case someone were to recognize me from the nonexistent "Missing" posters that are *not* circulating on the news right now. These are the things you think about on the run—where is the exit, what do I do if Darren walks in, would I be able to run away from my own mother if she came after me. And so on. I'm still careful. It's better to throw people off the scent, just in case.

I know you're wondering about this Mystery Guy. MG from now on. He doesn't live with me but he's here in the city. It would be weird for me to live with him because technically I haven't seen him yet. At least not in person. Soon, though.

Am I nervous? Yes.

I've turned my life upside down and that's partly due to him.

But I wouldn't have done it if I didn't think I needed to. I hope you know that. All this isn't just some whim or me being angry or an F.U. to Mom and Darren.

Shit.

Subject: A Day in the Life of Bea (Part Two)
From: Bea <b98989898@ymail.com>
To: Ezra <e89898989@ymail.com>
Date: Sun 14 Apr 12:03 CST

I heard voices in the market and it freaked me out. Surprise, surprise, it was not Mom or Darren or the police coming to search for a missing girl. It was Irene, stacking the shelves with new items, whistling to herself, parrot earrings jangling.

I wonder if you'd recognize me now. I feel less like a bug these days. Still bug-adjacent, but I'm changing back into human form. My hair is different and my clothes are different. I thought it was best to disguise myself a little on the off chance anyone started looking for me.

The market is open till 9 pm. I might stay till it closes or I might finish this and go for a walk down by the river. Yesterday I went to Scott Joplin's house, and you'd never know all that music was written inside it because it looks just like all the other houses around it.

I'm starting to feel like that. Like I can walk out of this market and up the street and down to the river or over to the art museum and no one will look at me twice except to think, *I wonder what that girl's so hopeful about?* Maybe someone will make up stories about me. Maybe they'll wonder where I'm on my way to and who I'm heading home to. Maybe they'll envy me and wish they had my life. I might even smile at them and say hi.

I meet MG tomorrow, and I don't know what I'll do until then. I feel like a kid, Ez. Like I'm Han Solo all over again. Like I really might just save the world.

Love,

Bea

Subject: Behind Closed Doors
From: Ezra <e89898989@ymail.com>
To: Bea <b98989898@ymail.com>
Date: Sun 14 Apr 13:35 EST

Your life sounds very . . . different.

Mine doesn't feel all that different.

You're going to have to let me know what this breathing thing is like. How does it work?

I am trying hard to be a good guest and not listen in on the conversation that's going on in the next room. But since the conversation is basically about me, it's really hard not to. I feel like a total jerk because Joe's in there with his parents explaining to them that I have nowhere else to go, and that it's their Christian obligation to let me stay here. He's even playing The Accident Card, and talking about how much you helped him recover, and how it's the least they can do to help me out in my own time of need. That's the exact phrase he used just now: *time of need.* He's much louder than they are, so I can't really hear their responses. One thing's for sure—he's not giving up.

I feel like a total jerk because it's this quality—the not-giving-up quality—that's been annoying me so much the past couple days. And now here it is, about to save me from going back to our house. Which I can't can't can't do.

I definitely see what you mean about Joe. Every minute, every second for him is a time of need. I'm not dating him, but I definitely think he's auditioning me to be his sidekick. I figured that since it was the weekend, I'd get to sleep late and chill out and think things over. Maybe, you know, breathe? But the minute he got up, he was getting me up too. You know why? To play video games. *For hours.* I've always thought that the whole point of video games is that they're something you can do on your own. And I imagine if I wasn't here, Joe would totally be playing them on his own. But since I'm here, it's video gaming as a social sport, with him giving a running commentary on every shot fired, every life point gained, every room entered. It makes him so happy to have someone to talk to, which is why I've been trying hard to get some happiness out of it too. But lord, sometimes I want a pause button.

Now he's asking them for *just another week*—that can't be a good sign, if he's trying to bargain for seven more days. But wait—now he's thanking them. I have to put this down so he doesn't know I've been doing something other than *Call of Duty* for the past fifteen minutes.

Subject: Behind Closed Bathroom Doors
From: Ezra <e89898989@ymail.com>
To: Bea <b98989898@ymail.com>
Date: Sun 14 Apr 13:53 EST

Hiding out in the bathroom now.

Here's the news:

There is no news.

Meaning: Joe came back to the room, picked up his controller, and resumed playing. Asked me what he'd missed. Then started telling me about this time he and Walter single-handedly won Vietnam in a single afternoon. Or something like that—honestly, I wasn't following. The point is—he didn't say a single thing about the conversation he'd just had with his parents. I was in the room when his mom asked if they could talk for a second. He knows this. But I guess he doesn't want me to worry. If it's just for another week, maybe he thinks he can get an extension. Or maybe he wants his sidekick around for as long as possible. No—that's not fair. He doesn't have to do any of this for me. I need to show more gratitude.

I also need to come up with a Plan B.

Thank you for letting me tell Terrence. I need his thoughts on this.

The big question is: How do I get out of this house without hurting Joe's feelings?

Subject: ????
From: Ezra <e89898989@ymail.com>
To: Bea <b98989898@ymail.com>
Date: Sun 14 Apr 18:53 EST

Mom called Joe's mom. It was like Mom's name was a dog whistle and I was a golden retriever—the minute Joe's mom said it, I was all attention. I paused the game Joe and I were playing, and at first he was confused, but then I gestured to the kitchen and he understood.

We listened in, and it soon became clear that Mom was calling to say she'd thrown Darren out of the house and was desperate for me to come back and make a new start.

KIDDING. What actually became clear was that Mom was accusing Joe's family of harboring a fugitive, and was demanding my return so I could be tried and executed. Darren was let out on bail, or maybe he was let go without charges—I couldn't tell, only hearing one side. Mom didn't dwell on that, only the send-Ezra-back-to-be-slaughtered part. I'll be honest—I thought Joe's mom would fold and say, "Sure, you can have him." But instead she surprised the hell out of me and stood her ground. She kept saying, "Now, I don't think that's a good idea, Anne. I don't think anybody's ready for that."

I wanted to run in and hug her. And at the same time, I felt so trapped. My whole life was being decided by two people who weren't me. Four, if you counted Joe and his dad. Five, if you counted Darren, who was no doubt standing over Mom, telling her what to say. I didn't want to feel so reliant. I didn't want to feel so dependent. I know this is stupid—I've been reliant on other people my whole life. But the trick is not to feel it, right?

Then Joe—*Joe*—said to me, "She's not going to kick you out. She won't send you back to them. She knows how bad it is over there. She understands."

But I haven't said a word. I haven't told him anything.

You must have. Because I could see it—he knows the lay of our land. At least a little.

I don't know what came over me. I heard his mom hang up. I knew I wasn't supposed to be listening. But I went right for the kitchen. Behind me, Joe said, "Hey!" but he couldn't stop me. His mom was standing next to the kitchen table, staring off. She didn't even try to cover it when I got there, didn't try to float a smile to her face, didn't try to change the subject that was suffocating us. No, instead she stopped staring off and looked at me, this stranger who was temporarily her responsibility.

I know that Joe almost died. I know his mom lived through that. But honestly that's not why I said what I said. I wasn't thinking about him at all.

"You're saving my life," I told her. "I know you don't have to, and I know it's a lot. If there's anything I can do to be less of a burden, I'll do it. But in the meantime, I just want you to know that you and your family are the only thing coming between me and a very bad reality. I am guessing that you know this, or else I wouldn't be here. But I wanted to say it out loud to you. So you know for sure what you're doing."

She nodded absently, then said, "You can stay here, Ezra, but it's not a permanent solution. I understand that you can't go back there, but you do have to talk to your mother at some point. Especially with your sister gone . . . you're all she has."

"She has her husband," I pointed out.

"Yes," Joe's mom replied. "But you're all she has outside of that man."

That man. Everything I need to know about why I'm living at their house is in those two words.

"Mothers worry," she added. "It's what we do."

I wanted to tell her that children worry too. Especially when their parents don't love them. Especially when they aren't given any real options. Especially when their own lives are too heavy for them to lift on their own.

"Aw, Mom," Joe said, heading over and giving her a big hug. "You're the best."

She hugged him back and I felt like I should leave, that even though it had been about me, there was still no place for me within it. I guess that's one of the side effects of growing up in a home that hates you—you have no idea how to act around love.

I mumbled a "thanks again" and got out of there. I went back into the living room and realized that this was my chance to leave—before Joe returned, before Joe wanted to hang out some more. So I left the house and started walking to Terrence's. I texted him to say I was coming. I texted Joe to say I'd left. Terrence texted back to say he'd be waiting. Joe texted back to say I shouldn't have left, because we were only two levels away from this awesome firefight.

I'm walking to Terrence's now—I'll spare you all the thoughts that are crossing my mind, since most are just variations of *What am I going to do now?* I hope that Terrence can get me closer to the answer without feeling he has to provide it outright.

In other words: I don't want him to think I'm asking him if I can move in.

More soon.

Subject: Good news, bad news

From: Ezra <e89898989@ymail.com>

To: Bea <b98989898@ymail.com>

Date: Sun 14 Apr 21:03 EST

I'm in the park now, stalling before I go back to Joe's. Things with Terrence aren't good. I'm going to try to get it down here—obviously, I'm not going to remember it word for word, but this is pretty much how it went.

When I got to his house, he was in his room, doing homework. I know his routines—he was just starting homework because all of the books and notebooks were open on his floor. (He won't put them away until he's done, so his floor gets clearer and clearer as he systematically completes everything he needs to do, usually left to right.) I laughed because there was barely enough room for me to sit down next to him—I had to slide his laptop over to make space.

"So I have some news," I told him. It felt big, to be able to have this conversation.

"Cool," he said, having no idea. "What?"

"I heard from Bea."

Now I *really* had his attention. He leaned toward me. "Wow. Where is she?"

I knew he'd ask me this. I just didn't expect it to come so soon. So I fumbled.

"Um . . . I can't tell you."

Now he sat back. Paused a moment before saying, "Okayyyyyyy. . . ."

"Seriously. I promised."

Terrence didn't seem happy about this. "You can trust me."

But that wasn't the issue. I had to make him see that. So I said something like I knew I could trust him—and I was sure that you trusted him too. (I could have quoted your email to him, but thought that would be weird.) I told him you were the one who'd told me it was okay to tell him I'd heard from you.

"I haven't told anyone else," I said to him.

Then he surprised me again by replying, "But you're going to tell Joe, right?"

I said that no, Terrence was the only person I could tell. I thought he'd be flattered that you knew I needed to talk to someone about it, and that he was the best person to talk to. I told him that. But instead of understanding or realizing how important this was, he said, "Isn't Joe going crazy, not knowing?"

I genuinely didn't understand why Terrence was making it about Joe.

"It's Bea's decision, not mine," I pointed out.

"Why did it take her so long to get in touch with you?" he asked.

I know what comes next is a lie. The only way I can explain

it is that I felt I'd already given a number of unsatisfying answers to his questions, and I felt that telling him we'd been in contact for a while would be the least satisfying answer of all. So instead I told him, "I just heard from her an hour ago. That's why I came running over here."

Again, he didn't understand how important this was. How before I had him, I wouldn't have had anyone—I would have kept it a secret forever.

"It's pretty mean of her to keep you waiting that long," he said.

I told him no, it wasn't like that.

But he wouldn't let it go. "Really?" he said. "Then what's it like?"

He was getting irritated and I called him on it.

"Why are you sounding so angry? Isn't it up to me whether I'm mad at my sister or not?"

"Sure. But you have to admit, a lot of the shit you're in has to do with her ditching you and leaving you alone."

I defended you. "First off, she had her reasons. And second, I'm not exactly alone, am I?"

That calmed him a little. He leaned back over to me, put his hand on my ankle. "No. You're not. But you know what I mean."

"Of course. You just have to believe me—it makes sense."

But even as he was being tender, he wouldn't let it go.

"Look, I like your sister. You know that. But you have to admit that she's not the most considerate person."

"What are you talking about?"

"I'm trying to help you here. Trying to give you some perspective."

"But what kind of perspective can you have? You have no idea what it was like in our house."

He took this as an invitation to say, "Then give me an idea! Tell me! You've invited me over, what, twice? Three times? I wouldn't even know your sister if she didn't give us rides. And yes, you've told me things—but you haven't told me everything."

I didn't understand how he could expect that. How anybody could expect that.

I said to him, "There's no way to tell you *everything.* Why would you ask me that? I told you about the time Darren made me practice answering the phone for two hours straight because he thought I'd answered it disrespectfully. I told you about being kicked out of the house and sleeping in the backyard because I hadn't finished my chores before bedtime. I told you how he instructed Mom not to get us birthday presents, because birthday presents only spoiled us—and how Mom went along with it. Don't you get enough from knowing *that*?"

"I'm just trying to understand."

"I know. And I appreciate that. But you *can't* understand. Nobody can understand. Nobody except Bea."

It's not a contest. I don't want him to feel like it's a contest. Because what kind of contest is it if he's never going to win, and doesn't even understand why that's a good thing?

Next he asked me if you were planning to come back. I hope it's okay that I told him, no, I wasn't expecting you would.

Then he said, "So she thinks emailing you is enough?"

"It's more complicated than that."

"Actually, I'm not convinced that it is."

I wanted to know where this was coming from. I asked him why he was acting all down on you.

He countered with, "Why won't you tell me where she is?"

I gave him as much of the truth as the truth would allow. "Because I can't."

"You can, Ezra. It's just that you won't."

"Fine," I told him. "I won't."

That got to him. I could see the words strike, could see him weaken for a moment, and knew I had done that to him.

He should have stopped it there. But he didn't. He pushed back harder.

"And it's not just that," he said. "There's something else you're not telling me. I know it."

I tried to halt the damage. I said what I thought would make it better. I told him, "If there is something I'm not telling you, I promise it has nothing to do with you. It all has to do with me."

Now he reached out and touched my arm, took my hand. Still tender, he said, "But you see, here's the thing: I thought we'd gotten to the point where something that has to do with you automatically has something to do with me. I thought we were at least close to that. It's how I feel. But maybe you don't feel the same way."

I pulled away—him holding my hand felt like a trick.

"You're twisting this into something it's not!" I insisted. "This has nothing to do with whether or not I care about you. Of course I care about you. And trust you. And love you. But none of that means I can tell you everything. There are going to be things I need to keep to myself. There are going to be things you can't understand."

"I won't be able to understand them if you don't tell me about them!"

"No . . . that's not what I'm talking about. I'm talking about the fact that you have this pretty decent family and this pretty decent life and there is no way to explain to you how wrong things can get when you don't have any idea what wrong feels like. I tried to burn my house down, Terrence. You would never do that, and you would never have any reason to do that. I can tell you about why I did it. I can try to make you understand. But I could talk to you for hours and hours and you still wouldn't know a tenth of what it feels like, how many things are going on in my head at once. I am giving you as much as I can, I swear. But that's all I can give. When I heard from Bea, you were the person I wanted to tell. This is where I wanted to be. You have no reason to be upset, or angry, or whatever it is you are right now."

I want so much to tell you he got it.

But he didn't get it.

He was hurt. And I was pissed that he was hurt. And he sensed that and got even more hurt.

It wasn't a fight. You and I have been a part of enough fights that I know this wasn't anything near a fight. But it was like after all these months of feeling like Terrence and I were getting closer and closer, I'd done something to point out that we were actually further apart than he'd thought. And once I did, it was hard to feel close again.

Do you want to know how I know Terrence is a good person? It would have been so easy for him to push me even further. It wouldn't have taken more than a few more words from him to turn the rip into something impossible to mend. Hurt puts your pride on the line, and I know the damage that can cause. I would have hurt him more, Bea, if he'd said the wrong words. But instead he said, "I guess the important thing is that your sister is okay, wherever she is. And you're not alone." Then, before I could respond, he said, "I need pizza. How do you feel about pizza?"

I told him he knew how I felt about pizza. Which made him smile and say, "Yeah, I suppose I do."

We got pizza. (His parents were out somewhere.) We sat on his family's lime-green couch and watched some Netflix.

The distance is still there, Bea. And I'm confused. I'm just going to let it all out here.

I think he might be the best part of me.

I think it's probably not healthy for the best part of me to be someone else.

I know I need his help.

I don't know how to ask for it. Because, let's face it, asking for help is not something we've ever been good at.

(That makes it sound like it's our fault. I know it's not our fault. If we'd ever asked for help, there would have been hell to pay, and that's the part that's wrong.)

I guess what I'm saying is—I know I'm sending him mixed messages. I'm telling him I need his goodness and at the same time I'm saying his goodness disqualifies him from really understanding what my life is like.

I know I need to figure this out.

You have to be feeling it too—now that you're out of the house, aren't you seeing more clearly how abnormal our normal was? Or maybe you saw it more at the time.

I'm going to go now and text Terrence and thank him for being there for me. I hope that makes him feel better and closer.

I also might ask him for some help with my homework.

He loves that. He pretends it annoys him. But I swear, he loves it.

Your abnormal brother,
Ezra

Subject: Get your head out of your navel, Ezra
From: Ezra <e89898989@ymail.com>
To: Bea <b98989898@ymail.com>
Date: Sun 14 Apr 23:36 EST

ME ME ME ME ME ME ME ME ME ME ME ME ME ME ME ME ME ME ME ME ME ME ME ME In ME ME ME ME ME ME ME ME ME ME between ME ME ME ME ME ME ME ME ME ME ME ME ME all ME ME ME ME ME ME ME ME ME ME ME ME ME ME ME ME ME ME ME ME ME ME ME ME ME ME ME my ME ME ME ME ME ME ME ME ME ME ranting ME ME ME ME ME ME ME ME ME ME ME ME ME about ME ME ME ME ME ME myself ME ME ME ME ME ME ME ME ME ME ME ME I ME ME ME ME ME ME am ME ME ME ME ME ME ME ME ME ME actually ME ME ME ME ME ME ME ME ME ME ME ME ME ME ME ME ME ME ME ME ME ME ME ME ME ME ME ME ME ME going ME ME ME ME ME ME ME ME ME ME ME ME to ME ME ME ME ME ME ME ME ME remember ME ME ME ME to ME ME ME ME ME ME ME ME ME ME ME ME ME ME ME ME ME ME ME ME ME wish ME ME ME ME ME ME ME ME ME you ME ME ME ME ME ME ME ME good ME ME ME ME ME ME ME ME ME ME ME luck ME ME ME ME ME ME ME ME with ME ME ME ME

ME ME ME ME ME ME ME ME ME ME ME ME ME ME ME ME ME Mystery ME ME ME ME ME ME Guy ME ME ME ME ME ME ME ME ME ME ME ME ME ME ME ME ME tomorrow.

Love me,
Ezra

I MEAN

Love, me,
Ezra

Subject: So . . . ?

From: Ezra <e89898989@ymail.com>

To: Bea <b98989898@ymail.com>

Date: Mon 15 Apr 21:12 EST

How'd it go?

Subject: Dying here. Hopefully not dying there.

From: Ezra <e89898989@ymail.com>

To: Bea <b98989898@ymail.com>

Date: Mon 15 Apr 23:17 EST

You realize I'm going to be afraid he was a serial killer until you tell me otherwise, right?

Subject: RE: Dying here. Hopefully not dying there.

From: Ezra <e89898989@ymail.com>

To: Bea <b98989898@ymail.com>

Date: Mon 15 Apr 23:19 EST

Or a kidnapper. Wouldn't that be ironic?

Subject: RE: Dying here. Hopefully not dying there.

From: Ezra <e89898989@ymail.com>

To: Bea <b98989898@ymail.com>

Date: Tues 16 Apr 01:01 EST

Going to sleep now. I better wake up to a full accounting of the evening's events.

Subject: Not dying here.
From: Bea <b98989898@ymail.com>
To: Ezra <e89898989@ymail.com>
Date: Tues 16 Apr 11:34 CST

Dear Ez,

Do you ever feel small? Like so small you could fit in your own pocket? Like as small as, I don't know, a baby, back when you had someone to cut your food and feed it to you? I wish I had someone to do that right now. Or bring me ginger ale and crackers the way Sloane's mom does when she has cramps or the flu, the way Mom never did, not even before Darren.

I feel so small, I wonder if I'm invisible. I feel as small as a flea. I'm looking at my foot right now, and there it is, but it's kind of a surprise to look down and see it because it's there and it's real and it's not small at all. (Also, my shoes are totally thrashed. I walk so much in my new life that the soles are wearing out.)

Why do you, my wonderful sister, feel invisible?

I'll tell you, Ez.

I am small and invisible and disappearing before my own eyes because I went to the Designated Meeting Spot yesterday, the one I have imagined and reimagined ever since I first knew I was coming here. I went there and stood with my heart beating out of my chest for everyone to see, and I wore a stupid, hopeful look on my stupid, hopeful face and I stood there for ninety-three minutes.

Ninety-three minutes.

Waiting.

For nothing.

For no one.

Because Mystery Guy didn't show.

Which means your sister, Beatrix Ellen Ahern, is an idiot.

We always knew it was true, right? Maybe you should tell Terrence. He'll love it. He'll be like, *I could have told you that.* Only he'll say it nicely with his hand on your ankle.

I know I shouldn't be mean.

That's what I do, right? Take my anger out on people who don't deserve it. I wonder where I could have learned that. The thing is, I really believed he would be there—Mystery Guy. I told myself, *Don't pin all your hopes on this, Little Mary Sunshine. Things don't always have a way of working out the way you want them to.*

But I went and believed anyway.

And of course he didn't come.

And I haven't heard from him.

And I am here in fucking St. Louis, Missouri, where my only friend is a woman with a collection of parrot earrings and an old Italian man who smells like garlic and has a forest of hair growing out of both ears, and my shoes have holes, and I've been wearing the same clothes for weeks, and I either sleep on a public bench or a hostel bunk bed, and buy my meals at gas stations—when I decide to splurge and eat—and I've started smoking when I can bum smokes off strangers because this is how stressed out—and, fuck it, *scared*—I am. And you know I can't smoke because I'm allergic, and smoking was what killed Aunt Lucy, and before that it aged her five hundred years by turning her face into a prune. So this is what I now have to look forward to.

Whatever you do, Ez, don't ever be like me. Be you. You're the best part of me. You always have been. You're the only good part of me.

And now there's nothing left. Just my ratty shoes, tapping under the desk, and now that I think about it, maybe my foot isn't real at all. If I took off that shoe, maybe there would only be air where my foot should be. Because I am smaller than a flea. I am nothing.

Bea

Subject: Maybe dying a little.

From: Bea <b98989898@ymail.com>

To: Ezra <e89898989@ymail.com>

Date: Tues 16 Apr 11:51 CST

Listen, we both know I can be Bea-centric, so here's my attempt at not being that on top of everything else.

I'm sorry about Terrence's reaction. I'm sorry I'm the cause of it. If I hadn't *left my life behind,* you all would be peachy keen and hugs and rainbows and fucking unicorns like always.

As usual, that's on me.

What's also on me: You now know Joe isn't all he's cracked up to be. If I'd just stayed *two more months* until I graduated, you wouldn't be a prisoner in someone else's home. You'd be a prisoner in our home, but at least your idea of Joe would remain intact. And it's nice to believe in people, isn't it? I've completely enjoyed the fifteen minutes of it I've known in my short, sad life.

Mom. Despite everything, there's this guilt. Maybe it's more the guilt of hurting someone I *want* her to be as opposed to the someone she actually is, but it's still guilt. At the end of the day, I have that at least, and my crap shoes, and this crap new hair I've given myself (think Kurt Cobain or Debbie Harry).

Do me a favor. Text Terrence right now. Tell him you suck

at all homework. Tell him you might fail if he doesn't help you. Tell him your academic survival depends on him. Let him know he matters. Tell him your sister is gone, but that doesn't matter. Terrence matters. Focus on that.

Give Joe a kiss. Or a hug, whichever will creep you out less. Tell him it's from me, that it's the hug you know I'd want him to have, you know, if you'd heard from me.

Be happy.

And don't burn down any more houses.

Although I do have to say, that was pretty fucking badass.

Love,

Bea

p.s. Believe it or not, there's also the guilt of not liking Darren. I know Mom loves him, for reasons we've never understood. I've tried to see something in him. Anything redeemable or lovable that could be the why of her loving him more than us. But I'll never get it, Ez. Never.

Subject: How Bea came to be (in a strange city miles from home)
From: Bea <b98989898@ymail.com>
To: Ezra <e89898989@ymail.com>
Date: Tues 16 Apr 12:36 CST

I could show you the emails. I won't, but I could. He didn't beg me to come here, but he made promises. *Promises,* Ez.

I just want you to know that I haven't lost my mind. That there's a reason I left our Indiana home for sexy, glamorous St. Louis, Missouri.

We've been talking for just over nine months. It started on a Sunday afternoon, which isn't usually when monumental things happen. Mom and Darren were out. You were out. The house was dull and peaceful, and I remember thinking: *What would it be like to live in a dull and peaceful house all the time?*

It was an accident, the way I found him. I tweeted some bullshit about being a prisoner in my own home, in my small town, and he tweeted back. And then, boom, there he was. Just like that.

I didn't answer him. You know how I am. And then he tweeted me again: *I know you're out there.* And I wondered if maybe he was psychic, or if there was some hidden camera somewhere in my computer, so for three days I didn't even get on Twitter, just in case he would know. I made out with Joe and hung out with Sloane and I drove you to Terrence's the night Mom grounded you. Remember?

And then I couldn't stand it anymore. He'd gotten under my skin, don't ask me why or how. So I followed him. On Twitter, not in real life. For forty-eight hours, he didn't respond, so I felt like the world's biggest asshole, but I still didn't unfollow him, and then in the forty-ninth hour, he did it. He followed me back. And I get this direct message from him saying, *There's more to life, you know, but it's like you tell yourself you don't deserve it. Why do you do that?*

And my heart is going a hundred miles an hour because this is the most insightful thing anyone has ever said to or about me.

So I write: *Maybe I don't deserve more.*

He writes back: *Why so angry?*

I write: *Because, well, life.*

Him: *So change it. Stop bitching and be the change you want to see in the world, Gandhi.*

Me: *Maybe I like being miserable.*

Him: *I don't think you do. I think some people do, but you're not one of them. You're made for bigger things.*

Me: *You don't know me.*

Him: *You're right. But I can put the pieces together.*

And then he writes: *I want to know you.*

No one's ever said that to me before. *I want to know you.* Most of the people I know make it clear they *don't* want to know me, and here is this guy, this stranger, who is taking the time to talk to me. It sounds pathetic, but I had to believe that he was who I thought he was, don't you see?

Even if I'm an idiot.

It's not like I decided to leave all at once. This may sound strange, but I don't think I really decided I was leaving until I was actually doing it. It hit me about fifteen miles from home. I looked out at the highway and I thought, *Huh. Look at you being the change you want to see.* I almost stopped the bus then, got off, turned back. But I didn't.

Franco is worried about me, I can tell. I asked him if I could help out at the store. I said, "You don't even need to pay me," even though I need the money.

He said, "Hmm."

I said, "I can stock shelves and keep things clean and help out with customers." He looked at my hair. My shoes. "Or organize the stockroom where no one will see me."

"Hmm," he said again.

I took this as a yes. I need to keep busy or I'm going to lose it. As in my mind. So I went straight to the back room, where he has piles of boxes just waiting to be unpacked. Where there are cobwebs in the corners of the ceiling. Where there is a stack of old photos of the store through the years—1933, 1945, 1960, 1978—edges curled yellow, just waiting to be framed. He followed me and watched as I scrounged through the mess for an old yellow step stool, which creaked when I unfolded it, as

I uncovered a broom, leaning behind the bathroom door, as I climbed onto the step stool and knocked out the first cobweb.

"Okay," he said.

"Okay?"

He held up his hands like *do I have a choice?*

"Great," I said. And then I hopped off the stool and held out my hand. He glanced down at it and the edges of his mouth twitched, threatening to turn upward. He put his hand in mine and we shook on it.

So it appears I have a job. Fifteen dollars an hour to start, six hours a day, six days per week. I'll be rich by summer.

Franco just poked his head in here and shouted a dinner invitation, and I know it's because I look thin and I've got crap hair and crap shoes and a crap life. I won't go because it's better not to depend on anyone, but for one horrible second I thought I was going to cry right in his face. He hates everyone except his wife.

I won't go back home. Not after everything that's happened. I don't want to go back anyway. I think the part of me that's still breathing would die and then that would be it, the end.

But what the hell am I going to do here?

Bea

p.s. Don't try to look up MG online. You won't find him on my Twitter profile because I deleted it. Sorry, Ez.

Subject: MG take two

From: Bea <b98989898@ymail.com>

To: Ezra <e89898989@ymail.com>

Date: Tues 16 Apr 17:21 CST

I'm writing from the library, where I'm sitting at a table stacked with books. Calculus. Physics. Anthropology. This probably sounds Boring, Boring, and Boring, to you, or maybe—overachieving younger brother that you are—it sounds like the ideal way to spend a Tuesday.

I worked all day at Franco's, and while it feels good to move around and keep my hands busy, my brain needs something to focus on. Otherwise all I do is fret and worry and ask myself what I did to scare Mystery Guy away. Or, alternatively, I sit in a fury and think of all the things I wish would happen to him.

So I am studying for no reason other than that I need a distraction and this library is the most beautiful place I've ever seen and these books were literally sitting here on this table when I sat down.

Did you know:

Human penises rely on blood flow to create an erection but other mammals actually have a penis bone?

Neanderthals were redheads?

If the sun were made of bananas, it would be just as hot as it is now, made of gas?

Events in the future can change what happens in the past?

Think about that last one, Ez. *Events in the future can change what happens in the past.*

What if all the things we do tomorrow—every choice we make, big and small—could somehow change our shitty, messed-up past? Would we suddenly become different people? Would we be somewhere else with some other family? Would Mom have stayed with our dad?

Or would we make our past worse than it was? Like, would Darren have been our actual father?

I'm not sure I like this idea. I want to, but it puts a shitload of pressure on tomorrow.

Subject: MG take three

From: Bea <b98989898@ymail.com>

To: Ezra <e89898989@ymail.com>

Date: Tues 16 Apr 18:04 CST

Okay.

Right after I sent that last email this came in. From Mystery Guy:

Something came up. Sorry. Let me make it up to you?

I want to say no, Ez, but I won't. I've come too far.

I wrote back: *Sure.*

One word, when what I really want is to write fifty-four of them: *Don't break my heart again. It's already been broken more than it can handle, so if you're planning to catfish me or stand me up again, just do me a favor and don't do it. Tell me now that this ends with poor Bea and her poor shattered heart so I can be prepared.*

At the same time I'm like: *Stupid Bea. Stupid trusting Bea. Go home. Finish school. Beg Joe to take you back. Be there for your brother. Don't turn your back on your mom. Admit you were wrong. Tell everyone you're sorry. Even Darren.*

At the same time I'm like: *Please, please, please let him be real.*

Subject: RE: MG take three

From: Ezra <e89898989@ymail.com>

To: Bea <b98989898@ymail.com>

Date: Tues 16 Apr 19:21 EST

What I really don't understand is why he called you Gandhi. Are you sure he really knows you?

Subject: RE: MG take three

From: Ezra <e89898989@ymail.com>

To: Bea <b98989898@ymail.com>

Date: Tues 16 Apr 19:23 EST

I know, I know—lame. I was just trying to get you to laugh. Right?

Subject: The view from here

From: Ezra <e89898989@ymail.com>

To: Bea <b98989898@ymail.com>

Date: Tues 16 Apr 19:29 EST

I don't know why you'd take any advice from me . . . but please be careful. The knight in shining armor might be great for a joust, and may have opened the gate to get you out of the castle—but he could be a complete fuckup once you get him off his horse. I don't want to be too down on him just in case he ends up being decent. But it's much easier to support someone with a tweet or a message. It's a lot harder to support them in person.

Meanwhile, Mom wants her purse back.

This time I wasn't called to the office. Southerly found me in the halls.

"Your mother called," he said. "She wants her purse back."

I actually snorted laughter.

"I take that to mean you still have it?" Southerly followed up. "She says she's canceled the credit cards, but it would make things easier for her to have her driver's license back."

"Clearly, I exist to make her life easier."

I had thought that Southerly might appreciate the humor of the situation, but he was stern when he said, “Watch it, Mr. Ahern. She is accusing you of theft.”

“If that’s the case, why don’t you ask her what she did with the money my grandmother left my sister and me? I’m pretty sure that when my dying Meemaw decided to leave us something for college, she didn’t think that meant paying off my *stepfather’s* college debts. Or his bail, for that matter. Tell my mother if she wants to play accusation poker, I’ve got *plenty* of good cards in my deck.”

Vice Principal Southerly, bless his heart, didn’t have a thing to say to that.

“I’ll return the purse and the license,” I assured him.

I didn’t add that I’d probably break into my own house in order to do it.

First, I need a lot of people to go to sleep.

Subject: Please tell me this isn't how love works
From: Ezra <e89898989@ymail.com>
To: Bea <b98989898@ymail.com>
Date: Tues 16 Apr 23:14 EST

Oh, man. Joe lost his shit tonight.

I guess I should have seen it coming. When something circles in the air long enough, you have to know it's going to run out of fuel and crash right into you.

When I got into his room he was just sitting on his bed, staring. Not in a Zen way either—more like shock. I tried to tiptoe past him, to the top bunk, but before I could get to the ladder, he said, "She never loved me, did she?"

"What do you mean?" I replied. "Of course she loved you."

"Not really. Not the way I wanted her to."

It didn't seem like the right time to give him a hug or a kiss from you.

He went on. "It's been three weeks, Ezra. *Three weeks.* Not a single word. If she loved me at all, she would have said something by now."

"She must have her reasons. . . ."

The look he gave me was poisoned. "Yeah—and the reason is that she doesn't give a shit about me. I never should have proposed. I fucking knew it would scare her—and that's exactly what it did."

I couldn't help it. I said, *"Proposed?"*

(I mean, really, Bea.)

"I didn't have a ring or anything. But I wanted us to promise to be together forever. I felt like we should do that. After everything we'd been through. Of course, you don't know about it—of course she didn't tell anybody about it. I think she was *embarrassed.* I was so upset that night, Ezra—the night of the accident, I mean. Not the night I proposed. The night of the accident, I really thought we were over, and I didn't mean to hurt myself, but I wasn't paying attention—and then when I woke up in the hospital, I thought, *You asshole. You almost killed yourself when all you want is to live with her.* I told her that—and for maybe ten seconds I thought she felt the same way. But she was never going to feel the same way. I get it. She didn't want to break up with the guy in traction. I probably knew that too. I went along with it, though, because it meant we were still together. Sloane warned me. She said Bea was using me. She said I was going to ruin my life over someone who wouldn't even look back at the wreckage once she was gone. This was before Bea actually left. But Sloane was right, wasn't she? Three weeks and no word. *Three weeks.*"

I tried. I said, "I'm sure she wouldn't want you to feel like this. I'm sure this isn't about you."

"How can you be so sure?" he asked. Then he gave me a long, hard look. "You haven't heard from her, have you?"

"No," I said, knee-jerk.

That's when I saw he didn't completely believe me.

"You wouldn't tell me if you did, would you?" he pressed. "The two of you were always thick together. You helped her, didn't you?"

"No!" I said emphatically. "I didn't know she was leaving any more than you knew she was leaving."

(True.)

"But she's gotten hold of you, hasn't she? All those texts."

"Those are with Terrence."

(True. But only because he said *texts.*)

"Then give me your phone. Let me see."

I was glad my phone was in my pocket, because I swear at that moment if it had been anywhere else in the room, we would have both lunged for it.

I shook my head. "No. You can't."

"Why not, if you have nothing to hide? I've been your friend, haven't I, Ezra? How 'bout you be my friend now?"

I started to back away.

"My texts with Terrence are private," I said. "I can't let you read them."

"I'm not going to read your texts from *Terrence.* I want to see your texts from *her.*"

The thing is—I always delete the history from my phone after I use it to email you, just like I do at school. But maybe he could trace it some other way—what the hell do I know about phones?

"There's nothing to see," I told him. "Nothing at all."

"I should have known you'd take her side! It doesn't matter how nice I am, how much I love her—there's no way of breaking through to either of you. Not even her. Not after all we've been through."

This statement pissed me off. "You went through one accident, Joe," I pointed out. "One accident that was *your fault*! She and I went through much more than that. *You know that.*"

Even as I was saying it, I knew it was the wrong thing. It was mean. Technically right but emotionally wrong.

But I finished saying it anyway.

Fuck, Bea—what if we really are our two parents' bad qualities rearranged into new people? What if that ends up being the best we can be?

He rushed at me then. And I guess I felt I deserved it, because I didn't move. I let him take me down. Let him gasp out, "Don't say that!" Let him shove me to the floor. Let him cry all over me because he couldn't wipe his eyes and hold me down at the same time.

"I'm sorry," I told him. "I'm so sorry."

And the pathetic thing?

I made sure to roll so that all my weight was on the pocket that had my phone.

He didn't go for it, though. Or at least not that I could tell. No, it's even worse. He just stood up and yelled, "FUUUUCK!" as loud as he could. Which was exactly what I wanted to do.

His father appeared in the doorway about a minute later. It wasn't that late, but he was already in his pajamas.

“What’s going on here?” he asked.

Luckily I’d already pulled myself into a sitting position.

“Doofus stubbed his toe,” I answered, gesturing to Joe’s bare foot.

His father winced. “Well, that’s never fun. But next time, maybe you could manage to say ‘Fudge’ for your mother’s sake. Or, Ezra, give him a pillow to scream into.”

“Will do, sir.”

After his dad left, Joe just shook his head at me.

“You guys are so good at that,” he said. “I hope you get some satisfaction out of fooling the rest of us.”

“It’s not like that,” I told him.

“Then what’s it like?”

“It’s like survival,” I said. “It’s exactly like survival.”

Now that I think about it, though—who did we learn it from?

If anybody asks, just tell them you fell off your bike and skinned your knees.

And I said, *But we don’t have bikes.*

And she said, *They’re not going to question that.*

I’m not going to think about that now. Joe’s asleep—Mom and Darren will also be asleep.

It’s time to break into our house.

There are things I need.

Subject: This is not how love works

From: Bea <b98989898@ymail.com>

To: Ezra <e89898989@ymail.com>

Date: Wed 17 Apr 00:13 CST

1. I don't feel good about this, Ez. Just throw the purse on the lawn. Don't go in there.

2. If you do go, PLEASE BE CAREFUL.

3. PLEASE DO NOT LET THEM CATCH YOU. But if they do, pretend you were sleepwalking. Remember how I used to do that? Until Darren tried to install a lock on my door—one that locked me in? Just say it runs in the family. That it's your turn now. Or, worse comes to worst, start screaming like Joe!

4. And speaking of Joe. I'm sorry I never mentioned the proposal, but to be fair, it made me feel enormously shitty. I mean, what kind of person tries to love someone and fails over and over again? Not just Joe, Mom, Darren, Sloane. But you. The only person I actually love in this world, and look what I've done to you. Turned you into an arsonist and a thief.

5. Which is why I hope this time it's going to be different. With Mystery Guy. I need it to be, Ez. I need to believe I'm not some feeling-less monster. Joe was wrong. I wasn't using him. I was *trying* to love him. There's a difference. The thing about me no one knows—even after all we've been through, I still believe, like truly, deeply, inexplicably believe, in love.

Subject: Thick as a thief

From: Ezra <e89898989@ymail.com>

To: Bea <b98989898@ymail.com>

Date: Wed 17 Apr 01:19 EST

First off, let me calm all your worries with a simple statement: THE PURSE HAS BEEN RETURNED. I'm sure you were deeply concerned about that.

Second, allow me to reassure you that a black Sharpie was taken to all forms of our mother's identification, and Darren's last name was crossed out on each and every one of them.

The photo of him she keeps in her wallet may also have been defaced. It's hard to draw a small penis and have it come across as a small penis and not, say, a dot, so I made sure to label it as a small penis.

As for the photos of us that she keeps in her wallet—well, I'm sure the reason I didn't find any there is because she would prefer to keep all photos of us close to her heart. That *must* be it.

Third off, I did not tamper with her pillbox or her feminine hygiene products. Because I am a gentleman.

Oh, and fourth—I didn't get caught.

I mean, all that aside—it was weird to be back in the house. I guess it would be the same for you coming back now too. It's not that anything's really different. (Though the scorch marks in the kitchen are a thing of beauty, if I do say so myself.) It's like you go back to the place and it's the same but you realize *you're* different. It was like walking through the past, not the present. And it's only been a few days.

She was somewhere in the bedroom. He was passed out in the den.

Our normal conditions for Staying Quiet.

Is it wrong for me to say that although I hated it as a home, there are still parts of our house that I loved? Like, it was never my room's fault that I was miserable. It never did anything wrong to me. If anything, it was the only space that allowed me to make it mine.

I took some clothes, but I couldn't take all of my clothes. I took three books, but I couldn't take the rest of them. I found some photos of us, and some photos of me and Terrence. That photo of you and me and Meemaw. Some shorts, because it's going to be summer soon.

I also unearthed my other big hiding place. There, in the pocket of one of my sweatshirts, this small plastic piggy bank. The kind you can open and close without breaking it.

I'd always meant to give it to you.

Subject: Confession

From: Ezra <e89898989@ymail.com>

To: Bea <b98989898@ymail.com>

Date: Wed 17 Apr 02:04 EST

No. I can't just leave it at that.

I think you understand. But that's a cop-out. I need to own it.

I need to say I'm sorry.

I'm sorry for never giving you that piggy bank.

I'm sorry for why I needed to get it for you in the first place.

I know I was only nine. But that's no excuse. I was so scared of him, but that's not an excuse either. When he asked who broke the lamp, I should have confessed and told the truth. But instead I pointed at you. I saw my way out and I took it. When you protested, I insisted even more. Because now there was the risk of being caught breaking the lamp *and* lying about it.

I didn't know what was going to happen when he marched us up to your room. I only knew it was going to be something bad. And what did he say—"You break things, you get things broken"—was that it? He knew exactly what to go for. You'd had that piggy bank, that ceramic piggy bank, since you were a little kid. And you'd never put a single penny in it, because there was no way to get the penny back out unless you broke it.

Which he did. Then he stepped on the shards for good measure, and told you that if you didn't pick up every single piece of both the bank and the lamp, he was going to smash another thing in your room, and he would keep on smashing things until all the pieces had been picked up. Who thinks of that, Bea? I'm not making this up in my head, am I? There are times I wonder if I have to be. And I also wonder if there are things I've blocked out.

The stupid thing is that it wasn't until tonight that I realized he was punishing us both. I thought it was just you. But he made me watch and didn't allow me to help. He had to know what that would do to me.

I felt so bad. I stole nickels and quarters from him and Mom for months, then bought the replacement piggy bank for you. Then I worried he'd see it and you'd get into more trouble for replacing what he'd broken. So I kept it hidden. And kept stealing when I could. From them.

I know it's stupid to apologize for this, six or seven years later. But that's what I'm doing now.

I guess that's the risk of going home—you find all this pain, with all this guilt mixed in.

But at least I have clothes now.

Okay, it's time for me to sneak back into Joe's house.

More tomorrow.

And I still owe you a piggy bank.

Love,

Ezra

Subject: A complication

From: Ezra <e89898989@ymail.com>

To: Bea <b98989898@ymail.com>

Date: Wed 17 Apr 02:09 EST

I think Joe's locked me out.

And I'm almost out of battery.

Shit.

Subject: Joe is a CHILD

From: Bea <b98989898@ymail.com>

To: Ezra <e89898989@ymail.com>

Date: Wed 17 Apr 01:16 CST

I hope he steals your phone and sees this email.

JOE, IF YOU'RE READING THIS, STOP BEING AN ASSHOLE!

I want you to bang on the door till his parents let you in. Joe may look like a nearly grown man, but inside he's *four,* and you cannot let him play these idiot baby games.

(Sorry if that sounds harsh, but I'm just So. Sick. Of. His. Nonsense. ARE YOU READING THIS, JOE? I HOPE TO GOD SO! We have real problems, Ez, you and me, which is something he's never understood. I get that everyone has their own amount of shit they carry around with them, and who am I to say ours is worse than his, but the truth is, it *is* worse than his. Plenty worse. So as far as I'm concerned, he can man the fuck up and open the door for you.)

DO YOU HEAR ME, JOE? MAN THE FUCK UP AND OPEN THE DOOR!!

Subject: A confession

From: Bea <b98989898@ymail.com>

To: Ezra <e89898989@ymail.com>

Date: Wed 17 Apr 01:23 CST

I'm going to sit here till I know you're inside.

Did I tell you Franco and Irene are letting me stay here? They said I can use the daybed and the adjoining bathroom (with shower!) and pay them $50 a month, which is only $20 more than the hostel costs *per night.* When I said, "I don't have any money yet," Franco said, "You're already working for it." And that was that. Franco and I both know he could charge more for this room, but he won't. Deep down, he's a big softie.

I made sure not to cry because he would have come undone and maybe even taken back their offer, so I just nodded like okay, thanks, and didn't make a big deal out of it. But it is a big deal, Ez. A really big deal.

Franco showed me the new boxes of olive oil and tapenade and crackers and olives that had come in and needed to be sorted. He showed me how to price them, where to shelve them, and how to work the old-fashioned cash register, which means we're at a whole new level of trust here.

And then he repeated his dinner invitation, but I said I was tired, and told him my little brother was in trouble and I had to make sure he was okay. I didn't mention that you were *breaking into our house and drawing penises on things.*

(It's nice, right? That he trusts me enough to give me the keys? We've come so far, Franco and I.)

I'm glad you got in and out without incident. Part of me wishes you hadn't been *so* much of a gentleman, and had actually done a little tampering, but I'm just grateful you're out of there safely.

Yes, I remember the piggy bank.

Like it was yesterday.

You don't need to apologize.

You were nine, Ez. *Nine.*

What were you supposed to do?

This is one of the things Mom and Darren have always excelled at—putting us in impossible situations. Situations that no one should ever have to be in, especially *children.*

So again, you don't need to apologize.

Besides, I have a confession too.

I should have told you before, and I'm sorry I didn't.

I want you to understand why I didn't.

This will sound stupid, but I was afraid if I told you—if I even said this out loud—it would go away.

I'm still a little afraid of that happening.

It's just that nothing good stays around for long, am I right? I had to make sure.

Technically, I still have to, but I figure I've come this far, and besides, I feel like I owe it to you.

The Mystery Guy is Dad, Ez.

It's Dad.

But wait, there's more.

He says Mom took us away from him. Not as in some custody battle that she won and he lost.

As in now you see us, now you don't.

As in we were stolen.

Which means this shitty life we've been living? It was never supposed to be ours. We were supposed to have a good life with a dad who loves us, here in St. Louis, Missouri. We were supposed to be nice kids in a nice family. We were supposed to be loved.

It's funny, right? In a really fucked-up kind of way. Everyone thinks I ran away from home when I'm actually running *toward* it. No wonder they aren't going on the news, begging me to come back. They're *kidnappers,* or at least Mom is.

I'm sorry I didn't tell you. I had to see him for myself first. To make sure. To see that he's not a Darren. That he's not Mom. I need to know he's a safe place.

I guess we'll put that physics theory to the test—the one about events in the future changing the past.

I'm meeting him Thursday—technically tomorrow. I'm sorry I didn't tell you. I'm sorry I didn't bring you with me. But if he's really who he seems to be—if this isn't some diabolical prank Mom and Darren have cooked up—then it might not be too late for us after all.

Subject: On the bright side

From: Bea <b98989898@ymail.com>

To: Ezra <e89898989@ymail.com>

Date: Wed 17 Apr 01:27 CST

At some point in our lives, Mom actually wanted us.

Subject: I don't know where to start

From: Ezra <e89898989@ymail.com>

To: Bea <b98989898@ymail.com>

Date: Wed 17 Apr 07:40 EST

There was a window open. I climbed through, slept on the couch, charged my phone, left before Joe woke up.

Then I started walking to school. Checked my email.

And this. Now, this.

I don't know where to start, Bea.

I'm just going to write.

Of all the secrets to keep from me THAT'S QUITE A SECRET TO KEEP. And also . . . WHAT?!? I know I wasn't even born when he left. I know you were only three years old. So our memories aren't the most reliable. But still—you're saying Mom kidnapped us? For no reason? So she could struggle alone for that many years? Out of SPITE? I'm sorry. No. That doesn't add up. Do you really think, all these years, we've been that hard to find? And then he direct-messages you on TWITTER?!? And bails on you the first time you're supposed to meet?

Remember that advice I gave before about the knight in shining armor?

IT APPLIES QUADRUPLE HERE.

I know you, Bea. I know you want me to be thrilled by this turn of events. I know you want this fantasy of yours to be true. I get it. Really. This is what you've always wanted—all those times the shit was really going down, you'd tell me he was out there somewhere, this better parent just out of reach. I liked that story . . . but it always felt like a story to me. Maybe it's because you were actually around when he was there—he held you, saw you, in a way he never held me or saw me—but I've never believed in him the same way you've believed in him. That might still be the case now.

I know you want to hear his side of the story. But please keep in mind: It's still a story.

I'm so sorry. Why can't I be happy for you? For us? Why can't I be thrilled by this news?

My mind is working overtime here. I won't lie. Because if what he says is true—if it wasn't his fault, if he's been out there all this time—I'm not sure it makes anything better. It might even make it worse. For me, at least. We got through what we got through because there wasn't any other option, Bea. To say that there was this other option the whole time—that kills me. And it makes me want to kill him too. Because I don't believe—I will NEVER be able to believe—that we couldn't be found.

I should put down this phone. I should let you do what you're going to do. I am so mad at you for not telling me, and for doing this without me. I have as much right to be there as you do, Bea.

I know you didn't cut me out in order to be mean or cruel. I know you love me more than that, and that you're making it up as you go along as much as I am right now. But still. I remember what you said about him—about how encouraging he is, about the freedom he's offered. About running toward instead of running away. If he's what it took for you to realize all that, sure. But don't leave one trap just to fall into another.

Why is it easier for me to think of you on your own instead of you out there with him helping you? I don't know.

I guess what I'm saying is this: Don't let him get away with anything just because you want him so badly to be what you've always imagined him to be. He does not get an automatic right to call himself our father just because we're carrying around some of his genetic material. Being our father is not an automatic position—it has to be earned. So make him earn it, Bea. If he deserves it at all.

And if he doesn't deserve it, find something else to run toward. Please.

Now, speaking of deserving—I need to go give Joe some hell.

Subject: ?

From: Ezra <e89898989@ymail.com>

To: Bea <b98989898@ymail.com>

Date: Wed 17 Apr 08:35 EST

Emailing you in class. Just to say I really can't believe any of this.

Subject: ???

From: Ezra <e89898989@ymail.com>

To: Bea <b98989898@ymail.com>

Date: Wed 17 Apr 08:37 EST

I also want to run screaming to Mom to ask her the truth.

Subject: Not exactly high noon
From: Ezra <e89898989@ymail.com>
To: Bea <b98989898@ymail.com>
Date: Wed 17 Apr 12:10 EST

So my big confrontation with Joe went like this.

Me: Dude, why did you lock me out last night?

Joe: Bro, I didn't lock you out.

Me: Well, when I got back from Terrence's, the door was locked.

Joe: Must've been my mom. Habit. She always locks the door at night, and had no idea you were still out.

Me:

In this pause, I'm deciding whether it's worth calling him on it. But that would mean moving to Terrence's house. And if I mess up there, then I'm out of options. Plus, after last night, I'm not sure how Terrence would feel about me moving in. I mean, he'd go along with it, and his parents would probably go along with it—but only for a day or two. So I make my calculations, and I say—

Me: No worries. My phone died so I couldn't text you. Next time I'll be sure to take a key.

Joe: Yeah, good idea.

So I guess I still have a place to sleep.

Subject: Just in case you think I'm thinking about anything else

From: Ezra <e89898989@ymail.com>

To: Bea <b98989898@ymail.com>

Date: Wed 17 Apr 12:35 EST

What time are you meeting him?

I'm dying here.

Subject: I am meeting him at

From: Bea <b98989898@ymail.com>

To: Ezra <e89898989@ymail.com>

Date: Wed 17 Apr 13:03 CST

4 pm tomorrow.

Subject: Okay

From: Bea <b989898898@ymail.com>

To: Ezra <e89898989@ymail.com>

Date: Wed 17 Apr 13:11 CST

I'm starting to freak out a little.

I know you're pissed, but I wish you were here, Ez. I don't have any nails left because I've chewed them all off.

I'm sure you're right that this is just *some fantasy* I've concocted in my stupid brain. Whoever I've been talking to could turn out to be some diabolically creepy old man or a bored housewife. But what if it isn't?

What if he's real?

Subject: Questions

From: Bea <b98989898@ymail.com>

To: Ezra <e89898989@ymail.com>

Date: Wed 17 Apr 13:19 CST

I used to think of all the things I wanted to know about him and from him, like:

- Why did you leave us?
- Was Mom always so shitty?
- Are you as shitty as she says you are?
- Do you know about Darren? Like, do you know how he treats your kids?
- Would you treat us like that, if you were here?
- What were you like when you were our age?
- Did you even *want* children?
- What are you most afraid of?
- What's the one thing you've always wished you could do?
- Which Avenger do you relate to most?

Don't laugh, that last one was really important when I was ten. I tried to imagine what his answers might be, and, more than anything, I wanted a dad who said, "I relate most to Bruce

Banner, not the Hulk version but the very humane, sweet scientist Mark Ruffalo version." Or maybe Steve Rogers or, of course, Black Panther, but that seemed too much to hope for.

I would tell myself, *Don't hold your breath. Don't aim too high, Bea.* Just like Mom and Darren taught us. *Be grateful for what you have.*

So then as I got older, I thought, okay, what if I had the chance to see him again and could only ask him *one* question? What would that question be?

It would be:

Why don't you want to be our dad?

Subject: My vow to you

From: Bea <b989898898@ymail.com>

To: Ezra <e898989898@ymail.com>

Date: Wed 17 Apr 13:29 CST

I, Beatrix Ellen Ahern (if that is my real name), do solemnly swear not to let Mystery Guy get away with anything just because I'm a sentimental idiot who wants her daddy back because all the other parents we've ever known are shit.

I promise to make him earn his right to be our father.

If he doesn't deserve that right, I promise to run toward something else as fast as I can. A brick wall maybe. Or an oncoming train. It will have to be something like that because if I don't have this, I don't have anything. I'm just a high school dropout runaway with nowhere to go.

Subject: Or

From: Bea <b98989898@ymail.com>

To: Ezra <e89898989@ymail.com>

Date: Wed 17 Apr 13:35 CST

I guess I could stay here and ask Franco to give me a permanent job. I can unbox crackers and olive oil and stock shelves for the rest of my life in exchange for a hot meal and a place to sleep. I can sing on the street now and then to earn extra cash, and read every book in the St. Louis Public Library. I can grow old here, and maybe one day, years from now, you and Terrence can come visit me, and you'll be all, *That used to be my sister, but now she's a sad, sad person I don't even recognize.* And you can spend an hour or two with me out of kindness before heading to dinner (I recommend Lorenzo's, even though I've never eaten there—Irene says it's "sublime"). Maybe you can even bring me something—breadsticks, maybe, or your leftover ravioli—and I will live for the rest of my short, sad, sad life on the memory of *the day my brother came to see me.*

Subject: Please do this one favor for your poor high school dropout runaway sister
From: Bea <b989898989@ymail.com>
To: Ezra <e89898989@ymail.com>
Date: Wed 17 Apr 13:41 CST

I know I dropped this bomb on you, and I know you're reeling, and I'm sorry, I really am. But let me have my fantasy, Ez. Just for another day.

And if you could maybe write back with something along the lines of a pep talk and not a rant, that would be nice too.

Love,
Bea

Subject: RE: Please do this one favor for your poor high school dropout runaway sister
From: Ezra <e89898989@ymail.com>
To: Bea <b98989898@ymail.com>
Date: Wed 17 Apr 15:12 EST

Okay.

Here's something you don't know. Or something you do know, but that we've never talked about.

Terrence wasn't the first boy I kissed. That first actually belongs to Jonny Pryor. A few of us were having a sleepover at his house—this was in seventh grade. The other guys had sleeping bags, and were going to crash in the rec room so they could play Xbox all night. Jonny said I could share his bed, and I thought, yeah, that sounded much more comfortable than a sleeping bag, especially the one we had, which looked like it had been used for shooting practice.

Anyway, we changed into our pajamas and got into bed. Almost immediately, I was like, *Something's going on here.* I became hyperaware of his body and I could tell he was hyperaware of mine. We said goodnight, and then just lay there awake for what felt like hours. Finally, after it felt like the whole house was asleep, he asked me if I was still up, and I said, yeah, I was.

"I can't see you—it's so dark," he said.

"I'm right here," I told him.

"Where?" he asked.

"Right here," I repeated.

He reached out, just like I knew he would, and touched my shoulder.

"Oh, there you are," he said.

I moved my hand, touched his shoulder, said, "I found you."

He moved his hand down my arm. I moved my hand to the back of his neck. And then, with the slightest possible movement, I encouraged him forward.

You can know something a long time before you can articulate it. You can want to say something a long time before you actually say it. At some point, I'd figured that if I was going to kiss someone, it was going to be a boy. But that was different from making it happen.

He kissed me first, but I pulled him into it, so maybe that counts as me kissing him first. It started just with lips, but became something that involved our whole bodies. Then, after a while, we settled into each other and fell asleep. When we woke up, we'd come apart, and I knew from the moment he looked at me that it was not something we were going to talk about or explore any further. He jumped out of bed and went to play Xbox with the other guys, telling me to come down whenever. I actually felt for a moment like it had been a dream, but then when I went down to the rec room and saw the way he was dodging my attention, I knew it had happened.

I didn't feel bad about it. I wasn't ashamed. I felt like I had wanted confirmation and had gotten it. Jonny had been the messenger, but the message was the important part.

It wasn't until I was walking home that afternoon that I started to feel afraid. The closer I got to our house, the greater Mom and Darren loomed. I felt they would sense it on me, a radiation emanating from my body. I knew they wouldn't approve—not just because I was gay, but because it was something I had determined for myself. They would see it as defiance. They would see it only in terms of themselves. And they would not be happy.

By the time I walked in the door, I was in a state of panic. It was almost absurd: Even though I knew they didn't love me, I was still afraid they would love me less.

I walked into that house and went straight to your room.

Even as I spiraled, the wiser part of me knew to spiral toward you. Even as I found a door to the brave new world and didn't feel brave myself, I knew you would stop me from doing the cowardly thing and closing the door completely.

You were not in the mood for company. You were blasting vintage Smashing Pumpkins and your door was closed. You were pissed that I walked in without knocking.

"What do you want?" you snarled, not even looking.

"Can I just hang out here?" I asked.

Maybe it was something in my voice. You looked at me then.

You looked, and you saw I had something in me that I didn't know how to hold. Somehow you knew not to ask me about it. Somehow you knew the best thing you could do was let me in and let me be.

This wasn't the first time I wasn't ready. And it wouldn't be the last. But what was true then has remained true ever since: Even when I was far from certain, I could be certain that you would be there for me in a way that nobody else in my life would be.

We never talked about that afternoon. You might not even remember it, because for you, it was just another Sunday. And for me, it was history being written.

Flash forward two years. I meet Terrence. I kiss Terrence. It's amazing. And while I don't exactly run home to tell you, there's no question in my mind that you will be the first person I'll tell about this boy who I really, *really* want to be my boyfriend. Because, when it all comes down to it, I need you for the good times as much as I do for the confusing ones or the bad ones.

This doesn't mean I won't rant. This doesn't mean I like being stuck here.

But it *does* mean you've always done right by me when it counted. And if you need to trust anything right now, trust that.

Good luck, Bea.

Ez

Subject: JONNY PRYOR?!!!!
From: Bea <b98989898@ymail.com>
To: Ezra <e89898989@ymail.com>
Date: Wed 17 Apr 18:01 CST

I remember you coming home. I remember the look on your face. I remember the mood I was in. I remember (god) the Smashing Pumpkins. I didn't know what happened to you, only that something *had* happened to you.

Oh, Ez. Looking back, I feel like a shitty sister. A really shitty sister. I've always been so in my own head about everything, and I'm not going to give a million excuses as to why that is because we all know what they are. For the past, I don't know, *life,* I've been so focused on building these walls around myself so that Mom and Darren can't get in, but the thing I didn't realize until right now, sitting here, at some nice old man's computer—some nice old stranger in a strange city—is that I've been keeping everyone else out too.

I wish I had asked you about that look on your face. Maybe it was what you needed, to be left alone, but lately I'm thinking we've had too much alone time in our lives. Too much of people just letting us be.

Thank you for being the only person in this world I like, much less love. Thank you for your email. Thank you for you.

Love,

B

Subject: But seriously, JONNY PRYOR?!!!!

From: Bea <b98989898@ymail.com>

To: Ezra <e89898989@ymail.com>

Date: Wed 17 Apr 18:05 CST

Huh.

Subject: My first kiss . . .

From: Bea <b98989898@ymail.com>

To: Ezra <e89898989@ymail.com>

Date: Wed 17 Apr 18:43 CST

. . . was Tripp Dugan. It was sixth grade and we were on a field trip to the Children's Museum, and afterward they fed us lunch in Hayes Park. Everyone was talking about what a baby thing it was, going to a *children's museum,* and I played along even though I secretly loved it. As in LOVED it. I still love that place. Everything is so hands-on and "this is how this works" and "this is where this came from" and "here, why don't you try for yourself!" It felt like the happiest place I'd ever been or could ever be. All of it so positive and interesting, and *encouraging* you to ask questions and be curious, not telling you to *shut up* and *mind your manners* and *don't be so stupid* and *if you can't be smart, be silent.*

But I was twelve, and worried about fitting in, and so I pretended it was a silly, baby place and I was so, so bored, and much too grown-up for something like that.

At lunch Tripp sat next to me. He said, "Wasn't that just the worst?"

And I said, "It really was." Kind of hating myself for saying anything mean about a place I actually loved. "I'm too old for baby things."

"Me too." And then he pressed his leg against mine under the table, and at first I thought it was a mistake, but then he kept pressing, and so I set down my sandwich and pretended to yawn like he was boring me too. All the while my heart was going, OHMYGODOHMYGODOHMYGOD.

He said, "You know what I'm old enough for?"

"What?"

"Sex."

It's amazing I didn't laugh in his face. But in the moment, Ez, it was *thrilling*.

I just shrugged, like *oh, sex, that old thing*.

He said, "I'm going to kiss you."

"Maybe."

"Don't you want me to?"

"I don't care if you do or don't."

He just smirked at me—remember that smirk he had? Back when he was younger? Before he turned mean? He said, "I'll bet."

He took his leg away, and I thought it was done, that I'd missed my chance, and part of me was relieved and part of me was sad. But then, on the way back to school, it happened on the bus. I sat in the very back, where I always sat, trying to keep to myself, and he came along and stood there for a minute and then dropped right down next to me. I knew then it was going to happen. He pressed his leg into mine again, and we rode like this for maybe a mile before he said, "What's that out there?"

"Out where?"

"Out the window." He pointed past me, and I turned to look, and then when I didn't see anything but trees and traffic I turned back and there was his face, right by mine. I think my eyes fluttered closed all on their own, and even as I was wondering why my eyes were doing that, he leaned in and kissed me.

It didn't last long. It was really just his lips against my lips. Mouths closed. Tongues well-behaved. Just a little exchange of pressure. But it felt momentous and enormous and like the biggest thing that could ever happen to anyone.

He never tried to do it again, not to me at least. (I found out later he was something of a serial kisser, which makes sense given the fact that he's gotten how many girls pregnant?) But from that day on I felt like I had this wonderful little secret, and somehow having that secret felt like protection. As long as I had that secret, they couldn't get to me, not really—Mom and Darren or the mean girls at school or teachers I didn't like or the world. I would be safe.

You're the only person I've told. In the scheme of things, I know it's nothing, but it isn't nothing to me. It's something. And it feels like the least I can give you right now.

Love,
Bea

Subject: Goodnight

From: Bea <b98989898@ymail.com>

To: Ezra <e89898989@ymail.com>

Date: Wed 17 Apr 19:07 CST

Franco needs to use the computer, so I'm signing off for now, little brother. Thank you for distracting me tonight. I'll write more tomorrow after I've met him.

God.

After I've met him.

I feel like I'm going to throw up.

I may actually throw up.

Okay, I had to run to the bathroom and throw up, but now I'm back, and poor Franco is worried about me. He says his sister Dorothea used to get sick to her stomach all the time, and they later found out she had some sort of parasite in her intestine. Can you imagine? That's all I need right now.

But it's really nice for a change to have someone care enough to worry. Other than you, I mean. I'm working for him in the market and I've officially moved into the office. So things are looking up.

Listen, no matter what happens tomorrow we'll be okay.

Right? We will. You and me. We've been through so much already. This is just one more thing.

We'll be fine.

Love,

Beatrix Ellen Ahern

Subject: With friends like these . . .

From: Ezra <e89898989@ymail.com>

To: Bea <b98989898@ymail.com>

Date: Wed 17 Apr 23:33 EST

I know you already know this, but let me state for the record once again: Our mother is a very strange woman.

Not only did she call Joe's mother again tonight to accuse her of harboring a fugitive (those were not her exact words), but apparently she also called Terrence's mom, which (according to Terrence) was *extremely* awkward because even though I've always been welcome over there as Terrence's "friend," Mom made it sound as if Terrence's whole family had swung me over to the gay side, and were therefore responsible for my deviant behavior in all regards—an accusation that Terrence's mom wasn't particularly equipped to counter. After she hung up, she called Terrence into the kitchen and basically asked him if I was planning on moving into his bedroom, to which he said no, no, absolutely not.

Terrence told all this to me over text, and ended the no, no, absolutely not part with a:

Sorry ☹

The amazing part is, of course, for all her ranting and raving, Mom hasn't called me once.

I guess she'd rather talk to Terrence's mom.

But, really, that's not the only thing I have to tell you. Because tonight I decided to go on a spying excursion. And you're going to be verrrry interested in what I found.

As you know, I've been experiencing Nonstop Joe these past few days. I'm pretty sure there's nothing much new he could tell me. But there's always been another missing piece: Sloane. She's still been treating me like I'm nonexistent in school. Even after Darren blew his fuse—not a word. I wasn't expecting congratulations or anything. Just recognition.

But she was avoiding me. She was definitely avoiding me.

So I decided it was time to throw myself in her way.

I couldn't ask Joe to drive me; if I did, I knew he wouldn't just drop me off. So after school, I just started walking.

I think it's safe to say that I took for granted all the rides I got from you. But I also have to say, there's something that calms me down when I walk places. It gives me room to think, instead of always feeling contained—by school, by our house, by a car. It makes me realize how much of my life I've spent hunched over, rushing by something I'm trying to avoid—Mom in the kitchen, Darren in the den, them both in their bedroom. Duck and cover. Don't make any noise. If that's your mindset at home, it can become your mindset for life. Rush by all the other houses. Rush through the halls of school. If you don't pay any attention to anyone else, they won't pay any attention to you.

Now, walking by houses instead of driving by them, I have time to wonder if maybe there are other houses like ours. Like, maybe the secrets are there, and they're just relying on us to not pay attention. I keep thinking about what you said about Jessica Wei. Why the fuck didn't I know that?

It has to be because I was rushing by. Right?

By the time I got to The Coffee Tree, I realized that instead of thinking about houses and rushing, I probably should have been thinking about what I was going to say to Sloane. She was behind the counter, like I knew she'd be. And it was pretty empty because, let's face it, Starbucks is still cooler than The Coffee Tree, and Starbucks is also much closer to school. There were a few people at the tables—senior citizens on the fourth section of their morning paper, and a few college students who were treating their tables like they were at a library.

Sloane was staring at the door when I walked in, so she saw me coming. She was already scowling, so it's not like I provoked that one. But I could definitely feel her throwing up the wall of silence, with a small slot left open for coffee orders. Her supervisor was standing right behind her—that older guy, Ray-MOND, who's always giving you your horoscope while the barista's waiting for the espresso to become pourable.

"Hey, man!" Raymond called out when I got to the counter. "What's your usual, and are you having it today?"

"Hey, Raymond," I said. "I'll just have a medium drip. And I'd love to have a word with Sloane too."

Sloane's scowl coalesced into a glare.

"I'm working," she said flatly.

Raymond let out a one-syllable laugh. "I think I can spare you for ten minutes so you can talk to your boyfriend here."

I could see how much Sloane wanted to scream FUCK YOU right in his face. But I guess after she got fired from Starbucks over Christmas, she actually learned how to speak to a boss.

"I only need two minutes," she told him instead. She didn't even bother to take off her apron. Instead she stormed out the front door. As I followed, Raymond yelled out, "Good luck, man! I'll hold your order until I see you survived this."

Sloane didn't wait for me in front; instead, she went by the trash cans on the side of the building. They smelled more like egg sandwiches than coffee grounds.

"What?" she said when I got there.

"I just want to talk," I said.

"So talk."

"Why are you being so pissy with me?"

"I'm not being *anything* with you, Ezra. I'm no longer obligated to put up with you, so I'm no longer putting up with you. I thought that was obvious."

"Okay, fine," I said. "That's fine. But I'm not going anywhere until you tell me what happened with you and Bea."

"Why don't you ask her?" she asked. And she got me, Bea.

She saw me thinking before I could say a word. So she immediately pressed on with, "You've talked to her, haven't you? That's so fucking typical."

"I haven't *talked* to her," I spun. "And why is that typical?"

It is entirely possible that I don't know the difference between the way scorn and pity look on a person's face, because I swear to god, Bea, I couldn't tell which one was dominating as Sloane glared back at me.

"Your sister's a user, Ezra. Which means she always needs someone to use. She's run out of any power she had over me, and she's grown tired of sucking all the life out of Joe, which leaves . . . you. Because I'm not sure if you've noticed, but she didn't have any other real friends. I wonder why that is?"

Even though I knew you'd left her—even though you'd told me you were worried about your friendship—I wasn't expecting her to be so cold when she talked about you. She's the only person who ever came to our house as a friend, the only person who ever joined you in stepping through the minefield, even after she knew there were mines there.

"What happened?" I had to ask. "You were like sisters."

Sloane sighed. "Yeah, well—not all sisters talk to each other when they get to be adults. That's just life."

"I know you're pissed she left. I'm pissed she left. But—"

"No," Sloane interrupted. "To be pissed, I'd have to be surprised. But I saw this coming."

"What do you mean?"

"I mean, I'm not stupid. I can tell when someone's keeping a secret. And things with your sister and me? It used to be that when I saw that she had a secret, I could also figure out what the secret was. Because there weren't the walls there. Then suddenly, she was building the walls. And the most fucking offensive thing of all is that she thought I didn't notice. So I let her have her walls. I was sick of everything being on her terms. And, frankly, I was sick of seeing Joe fall for her act too, even if he refused to see it himself."

"But you don't talk to Joe anymore either, do you? Why not?"

"Because he's only going to want to talk about her. And I want to change the subject. That's what she wanted. And it's something I'd strongly suggest you do too."

"Look," I said, "I'm *trying*."

Only *said* is the wrong word here. When the words came out of my mouth, it was like I was that annoying ten-year-old brother again. I was *whining*.

And this, of all things, got through to her. For just a moment.

"I know," she said. "I get it. And when I heard that you'd gotten out of your house—I'll admit it, Ezra—I fucking cheered. I thought, *There's hope for him yet.* But you have to do the same thing with Bea, before she drags you down too."

"How did she drag you down?" I pressed.

Sloane shook her head. "Nope. Time's up. You've gotten all you're going to get from me. I'd tell you to ask her what happened, but all you'll get is a lie. That's how it is. Now—I don't want you pulling this shit again. Leave me alone and I'll leave you alone, okay?"

(Those were her exact words: *Leave me alone.* It was only on the way home that I thought—we say this all the time, but who the hell really wants to be left entirely alone?)

I looked for a way to argue. I wanted to appeal to something in her, something that would make her talk to me more. But also, I kind of got it. If she was through with you, she was through with me too.

"Don't come back in," she said, straightening her apron. "I'll tell Raymond you canceled your order. If you want coffee, go to fucking Starbucks, or pick a time I'm not here."

That was it. I can't say it helped much. I guess I'm certain now of how angry she is, and that things went bad. But I'm still unclear why.

And as for her warning me away from you—well, I'm writing all of this to you now, right?

I know this is all over the place. I got home in time for dinner with Joe's family, and that's when Mom called, and then Terrence texted to tell me that Mom called there too, and then I played video games with Joe for a couple of hours and did homework for considerably less time, and now everyone else is asleep and I'm downstairs, and I'm sure one of the reasons I'm thinking of all of these things at once is because I'm not letting myself think too much about you meeting our father tomorrow. I know you're really hoping he shows up, and I guess you've got me hoping he shows up too, if only because I also want answers, Bea, even if they're only half-answers or answers that reveal themselves in the form of lies for us to disprove.

So yeah. Good luck. Let me know how it goes.

I love you in a way that Sloane clearly doesn't anymore,

Ez

Subject: Sloane

From: Bea <b989898989@ymail.com>

To: Ezra <e89898989@ymail.com>

Date: Wed 17 Apr 22:57 CST

This is so typically Sloane.

So Franco has gone home and I'm waiting to see if I hear from my little brother once more before I sign off for the night, because, you know, I'm meeting our father tomorrow after fifteen years and I'm chewing past my fingernails into the actual skin of my fingers and I've thrown up again, and I should probably try to get at least a few hours' sleep.

I'm going to paint you a picture, Ez, because it will be the fastest way to do this.

The part of the Best Friend will be played by Sloane. The Boyfriend by Joe. The Villain, of course, by me.

The time is last December. The setting: Bradley Hoyt's holiday party. You know how much I love parties—especially high school parties—and by *love* I mean I hate them with everything I am. But Best Friend said, *Come on, Bea, just this once, you never do anything I want to do, you're always in your own mind, lost in your own world, consumed by you you you, the least you can do is go to this fucking party with me.* And on and on until I decided to play nice because I can't afford to lose Sloane too, right? And so I went to the fucking party.

Only I was late because that was the night Darren decided to take all the presents from under the tree and relocate them to the driveway. You remember the great Christmas Present Trample of Last Year. Not that there were a lot of presents, but did he have to run over all of them?

Anyway, I wasn't exactly in a party frame of mind, but you were with Terrence, and Sloane and Joe were both at Bradley's, and there was no way I was staying home.

So, like you, I walked. Because sometimes walking is the only thing that makes sense. And by the time I got to the party, Best Friend was nowhere to be found. And Boyfriend was nowhere to be found. But I'd come all this way, don't you see, and what reason did I have to go home? To watch Mom clean up all the wrapping paper and ribbons that were blowing around the yard? To watch her peeling shit off the driveway?

So I stayed, and I had a drink, and I talked to Bradley Hoyt's idiot friends, and I stood there like a regular, normal, ordinary person with a regular, normal, ordinary home life—someone whose presents currently sat under the Christmas tree instead of smashed into the concrete—and I thought, *This is easy. I should do this more often.*

I pretended I was Bea Ahern, just a regular girl. I laughed and chatted my stupid face off, and I could see how surprised they were, Bradley and all his friends, as if I was an animal believed incapable of making human conversation until that very moment. You should have seen me.

At some point, I went in search of the bathroom, and that's when I found them. Best Friend and Boyfriend. Sitting in that room Bradley's parents use to store all the workout equipment they don't use. Best Friend was perched on a treadmill and Boyfriend was sitting at her feet. Only they weren't doing what you'd expect them to be doing. They weren't in the throes of some illicit passion. I didn't walk in on them naked. I didn't even walk in on them kissing. I walked in on them talking about me. About how selfish I am. About how I always let everyone down. How I say I'll meet you at a party, only I don't show. How I say I'll love you forever, but then I try to break up with you. How even when I tell the truth about the land mines, I'm a liar because I'm a shitty and disappointing friend who can't ever seem to put herself aside long enough to think about what other people might be going through. I mean, sure the land mines are bad, but I'm not the only person in the world with land mines to deal with. Best Friend has them. Boyfriend has them. Maybe not the same land mines. Maybe not to the same degree. But does that keep them from being there for others? No. Does that keep them from being on time to parties? No.

And then they did kiss, which is so cliché, and from where I was sitting it was pretty sloppy, like two dogs licking each other's faces. But that's not what bothered me. I couldn't have cared less about that stupid kiss. What I did care about was listening to the two people closest to me—next to you, that is—talking about what a shit I am. I mean, it was pretty nice for a while, believing that someone in this world other than you, my own brother, believed I wasn't all bad.

So I left the party. At least I walked out. Into the night. Into the cold. I sat in the yard for a while because I didn't want to go home. I think I texted you. Did I text you? I can't remember. I wanted to.

So I sat.

And I sat.

And I waited, but I wasn't sure for what. Maybe for enough time to pass so that I could go home and home would be different and the presents would have magically reappeared under the tree and Mom would say, "There you are. We were worried about you. Come in out of the cold and let me fix you something hot to drink," like she did sometimes when we were little, back before Darren.

I was still there, outside Bradley's house, when it happened. The stuff that came after. Sloane making out with Reggie Tan, and Reggie going back to school and telling everyone she slept with him when she didn't because she's waiting till college. That's what Sloane blames me for most. Because if I had been there, Reggie wouldn't have happened because she wouldn't have been drinking, not as much anyway, and she wouldn't have been mad and she would have been having the time of her life. And my not showing up wouldn't have left her on her own. Again.

And I'm not lying. Don't you think if I were I'd think up something better than this?

The truth is always sadder than lies anyway. Smaller and sadder and so much more complicated. Just like real life versus fiction. Just like us.

Small, sad us.

I'm going to bed now. You can believe Sloane or you can believe me, Ez, I really don't care.

Except that I do care. I'm just too tired right now to try to win you over to my side again.

Love,

Bea

Subject: THE MORNING OF

From: Bea <b98989898@ymail.com>

To: Ezra <e89898989@ymail.com>

Date: Thurs 18 Apr 08:29 CST

I was up at five. After staring at the ceiling and chewing at the skin where my fingernails used to be, I finally got out of bed and got myself ready. I even put on makeup and attempted to do something with my hair, and then I went out into the store.

I worked on the unboxing and pricing, first the olive oil, then the tapenade, then the crackers, then the olives. Each bottle, each jar, each package was so beautiful. I handled them delicately, like they were diamonds. Most of them had traveled from far away. I thought of closing myself up in one of those boxes and sending myself to Italy, to New York. I imagined being unboxed in a place with noise and life and color and electricity, and all these strangers who didn't know me, who didn't know anything about my former life. I set the jars and the bottles and the packages one by one on the shelves where they belonged and thought about how far they'd traveled to get here, just like me. It was a very reflective moment for me, Ez. You would have been proud.

Then I found a broom and swept the entire place, corner to corner, and the whole time I pretended I was sweeping my old life away. I swept and swept, and then I got down on my hands and knees with paper towels and Pledge and crawled around on all fours scrubbing away—goodbye Mom, Darren, Joe, Sloane, the old Bea—till the wooden floors shone clean.

At some point the lock in the door turned, and in came Franco. He stood blinking at me, at the shelves, at the floors, and then he nodded. He held up a white bakery bag and said, "Come eat."

We sat on stools behind the long wooden counter and ate donuts, still warm from the shop. Franco's eyes traveled around the store, and I watched him as he took in the neatly stocked shelves, the shine of the floors, the way they gleamed in the early morning light. Seriously, Ez. I'm a messy (okay, slobbish) person, but you know how cleaning helps me think. Well, this was some of my best work. It was my way of thanking him and Irene for believing in me and for taking me in without actually *saying* it, which would have made ol' Franco run for the hills or maybe boot me back out onto the street.

I ate donut after donut. Finally he nodded at the store and his eyes left the shelves and the floors and settled on me. "Very nice," he said. Short but sweet.

We ate for the rest of the time in silence. And it *was* very nice. All of it.

Whatever happens today, Ez, I love you too.

Subject: ALMOST THE AFTERNOON OF

From: Ezra <e89898989@ymail.com>

To: Bea <b98989898@ymail.com>

Date: Thurs 18 Apr 15:49 EST

I don't know how I'm going to look at Joe now without punching him in the eye. Or the balls.

Which you don't need to be thinking about right now. Or any of what I'm about to say. Mostly I'm just saying it to get it out of my head. Mostly I am very aware that the next time you write to me, you'll have news about our father. Or not. Depending on whether he shows.

Putting aside all the shit that you've just thrown my way re: Joe and Sloane, there's something she said to me yesterday that is sticking with me—it's the thing I want to get out of my head. Because as I walked around school today, I kept thinking this:

Why don't I have more friends?

I mean, I'm not a total loner. I have Terrence. I talk to him all the time. And after that, there's

What I'm trying to say is, when I'm talking about people I actually talk to, not just people I sit with at lunch, there's Terrence and then there's

My good friends,

Shit.

I'm walking through the halls today, seeing all these familiar faces, but then I'm asking myself how familiar their *lives* are to me. It's not like I don't pay attention. I know who's dating who. I know who's going to spout shit in class and who's going to stay silent. I know which kids will get called on and which ones get picked first in gym. I generally know who will end up sitting where in the cafeteria.

But that's not friendship.

Especially when I ask myself how much they know about me.

Which all leads to me asking:

Have they spent all these years hiding from me? Or have I spent all these years hiding from them?

I don't even feel I've been lying to them. I just created so much distance that no one could ever ask me the truth.

Terrence has plenty of friends. Church friends. Childhood friends. Yearbook friends. Track friends. And none of them seem to mind when I come along. But except for five-minute conversations in the halls or while we're all out together, it's not like I'm ever alone with them or know them as me, not as Terrence's plus-one.

I can't see any way to bring this up with Terrence without pushing him away more. He feels bad about what went down with our moms, and how his family is now guarding itself against me. (That's not how he put it.) He keeps saying things like, *We'll get through this* and *I can talk to them* and *You're always welcome, no matter what they say.* It's sweet—I know it's sweet. But it's like he's rallying around a flagpole that's missing its flag. I'm standing outside the rally, with the flag caught in my throat.

As I'm wondering how I managed to get to be fifteen years old without having fifteen friends, I see Jessica Wei at her locker, switching her books before lunch. And I think: One way to prove that I'm not hiding is to actually step toward someone else.

She doesn't act like it's unusual for me to be hovering over her. In fact, she acts like she was waiting for me to show up.

"How's it going?" I ask her.

"Not bad." She closes her locker, looks at me. "The question is: How about you?"

"I'm completely messed up," I tell her. "I'm not sure I have anywhere I can live. And, let me tell you—that sucks."

And Jessica, who doesn't really know me at all, says, "Fuck. I figured it was bad, but I didn't know you were homeless."

My first instinct is to protest. Tell her no, no, no, no, no—*homeless* is an old man who hasn't showered in weeks, pushing a shopping cart full of bottles. *Homeless* is a family whose house has been ripped apart by a tornado. *Homeless* is a queer teen kicked out of their house because of who they are, and forced to live in a shelter, or under a bridge, or in the back of a car.

I am not homeless, I say to myself.

But then I ask myself back, *So what are you, then? Where is your home?*

Which makes me realize: I am homeless.

I haven't had a safe home for years.

Now I have no home.

Jessica doesn't act like it's strange that I'm lost in my head for a minute while she's standing there. When I come back, I start to apologize, and she tells me not to. I don't have to. There's no need.

The problem is, at that moment, Serena shows up, asking what's taking Jessica so long. Serena asks this with me standing right there. It's clear I'm the thing that's taking her so long.

Childishly, I want Jessica to tell Serena to leave us alone. But Serena is Jessica's good friend. Maybe her best friend. I, meanwhile, am no one and nothing to her. What right do I have?

Jessica tells Serena she'll be right there. Serena, satisfied, heads to the cafeteria.

Jessica turns back to me and says, "Come have lunch with us."

I shake my head and tell her I can't.

She asks me why. And I say, "If it were just you, I totally would." Then I realize how awful that sounds and add, "Which isn't anything against Serena and your other friends. They're fine. But I can't say the same things to them that I can say to you. Not that you're under any obligation whatsoever to listen to me. I know I'm, like, a stranger. Or kind-of a stranger. I mean—we're not friends, exactly. And you should be with your friends."

I'm telling you, Bea—it was pathetic. Like I'd forgotten how human beings are supposed to act in social situations.

But instead of running away, Jessica says, "No, I get it. And honestly? If there was any way to blow them off, I would. It's just that we have a project due sixth period that isn't near ready to be handed in, so I need to be there. But look—how about we get coffee after school tomorrow? Just us."

"Sure," I say, trying to hide (hide!) my disappointment. I need a friend now, not tomorrow afternoon.

Though that's stupid too. Because what am I going to say to her? *Hey, you don't really know me, but I am losing my mind, in no small part because my runaway sister might be meeting our runaway father in a few hours, so it's like this huge part of my life is happening thousands of miles away from my body.*

No. I don't think so.

The only person I can say that to is you. So here I am, saying it.

My life?

It's going to be on hold until I hear back from you.

At this point, I don't even care how it plays out. I just want it to be past tense, so we know what it is, and can figure out how to deal with it.

Good luck,
Ezra

Subject: Hello
From: LONDON WOOSTER <l89989889@ymail.com>
To: Ezra <e89898989@ymail.com>
Date: Thurs 18 Apr 20:03 CST

Dear Ezra Ahern,

My name is London Jonathan Calvin Wooster. I'm fourteen years old (almost fifteen!), and Bea told me to write this. I'm the one who's been contacting her. It's my fault that she left home two months before graduating high school, and it's my fault that you set your house on fire and had to go live somewhere else. I sent her the messages and asked her to come out here. I thought she'd bring you too. I'm your brother.

I'm sorry.

Sincerely yours,
London Wooster

Subject: Hello again

From: LONDON WOOSTER <l89989889@ymail.com>

To: Ezra <e89898989@ymail.com>

Date: Thurs 18 Apr 23:21 CST

Dear Ezra Ahern,

It's me again, London Wooster. I know you don't know me, and I'm sorry to drop this crap bomb on you, but I figure the best way to get through this catastrophe is to try to explain.

I'm your brother. Technically your half brother. Surprise! I'm writing to you because Bea has taken off and I don't know where she's gone or if I'll hear from her again and there are some things I think you should know.

There's no good way to say this. I'm trying to imagine how I'd feel if I got an email like this from someone I didn't know. I'd probably be like F you, and maybe stop reading. Except that I'm naturally curious, so I probably wouldn't stop reading.

I hope you won't stop reading. This is pretty much the scariest thing I've ever done. Writing to you, I mean. The stupidest thing I've ever done is this:

A few months ago I wrote to Bea pretending to be our dad.

It took her a while to write me back, but then she did and we started talking. I couldn't believe it! At some point I told her I was dying. Not actual me but Dad me. I didn't even plan it, it just came out. And before I could change my mind it was out there. And then she said she was coming to see me before it was too late because she wanted to know me, and I kept not saying anything to stop her, and I may have told her that I was dying immediately. And then she actually showed up!

The thing about my dad—our dad—dying wasn't a total lie. He died last year from a heart attack. He was a good dad. I'm not saying that to make you feel bad. But he was. He was maybe the greatest dad, but then I don't have anything to compare him to and that's not, like, based on scientific knowledge or anything. I just really loved him. And I miss him. All the things I wrote to Bea about him were true. He wished on 11:11. He never made left-hand turns. He didn't pick up pennies for good luck because he said he was already lucky, so he left them for other people. Those are just a few of the good things.

So I'm really sorry about the crap bomb, but in some ways, I think I kind of know how you feel. Because I just found out about you. I was going through boxes. All these boxes of his stuff. And there you were. Actually there Bea was. Jumping off the pages of his journal where he wrote all about this second family he never ever mentioned! The detectives he hired. The ones that discovered your sister was living in Indiana under the name Beatrix Ahern.

You weren't in the journal. I found out about you from Bea. I'm not sure Dad ever knew you existed.

I'm sorry about that too. I feel like in some way it's my fault because your mother, Anne Wooster, left him after he got my mum pregnant with me.

Apologetically yours,
London Wooster

Subject: Some things about me

From: LONDON WOOSTER <l89989889@ymail.com>

To: Ezra <e89898989@ymail.com>

Date: Fri 19 Apr 08:12 CST

Dear Ezra Ahern,

My friends call me Lo. Not that we're friends and not that I'm assuming we ever will be, but I just wanted you to know you can call me that if you want.

Or maybe you'll think of another name, which is cool too. I've always wanted a unique nickname. My best friend, Thomas Warmflash, has been Wormy since second grade. And my friend Megan Louise Vanacore is Midge to her family, The Meg to Wormy and me, Vanna to her girlfriend, and Lou to everyone else.

Other things about me:

I'm sneak-writing this on my phone, sitting in this gnarled-up oak tree outside my bedroom window. When I was seven I named it Captain America because it was big and strong and seemed kind. That probably sounds crazy. But then I'm sure all of this sounds crazy to you.

My mom's name is Amelia and she's a landscape architect. So

I know a lot about plants. (Most people call her Ames for short, but our dad called her Amélie, like the movie.)

From Captain I can see all the way to the river and the arch.

I'm in ninth grade.

I'm going to send you a picture of myself so you can see if we look alike. Bea and I have the same nose, which is our dad's nose. She took one look at it and said, "So you got it too. I'm sorry."

I have a dog named Mustache. He's six.

When I get older I want to be an archeologist. Dad used to take me to watch these digs sponsored by the university, and sometimes they would let me help out.

I'm good at digging.

I've never had a brother before but I've always wanted one.

Sincerely yours,

Lo

Subject: One more thing

From: LONDON WOOSTER <l89989889@ymail.com>

To: Ezra <e89898989@ymail.com>

Date: Fri 19 Apr 20:48 CST

Dear Ezra Ahern,

I should probably stop writing to you because I don't want to overwhelm you or anything, but I just wanted to say again how sorry I am.

I hope you'll think about writing me back. I'll hang out in Captain till you do.

Your brother,
London

Subject: Last one, I swear

From: LONDON WOOSTER <l89989889@ymail.com>

To: Ezra <e89898989@ymail.com>

Date: Sat 20 Apr 00:52 CST

Dear Ezra Ahern,

Actually I'm not really going to hang out in Captain all night because it's not that comfortable and I have to be up early for a dig at Sappington House, the oldest brick house in the county. Also Mom would kill me. And what if you don't write back for hours or ever? I'd be up here for a long time and I'm sure I'd get hungry.

So goodnight, Ezra. And if you decide not to write me back, goodbye. I'm sorry I didn't get to know you. And who knows? Maybe you'll be sorry you didn't get to know me too.

London

p.s. I didn't mean that in a threatening way. I just meant that maybe you've always wanted a brother, like I have, and here I am.

p.p.s. I wish I could climb back into the TARDIS and do it all differently, but in some weird way I felt like meeting you would be like holding on to a piece of Dad.

Subject: FW: Last one, I swear

From: Ezra <e89898989@ymail.com>

To: Bea <b989898898@ymail.com>

Date: Sat 20 Apr 02:12 EST

Bea,

Please tell me what's going on. I need to hear it from you, because I don't trust anything else.

Ez

Subject: FW: Hello

From: Ahern, Ezra

To: Hall, Terrence

Date: Sat 20 Apr 07:24 EST

Terrence,

This is what's going on with me this morning.

No one else is awake yet here, but they will be soon. I have to get out of here.

I don't know what to do. But at least you now know what's happening.

xoxo,

Ezra

Subject: RE: FW: Hello

From: Hall, Terrence

To: Ahern, Ezra

Date: Sat 20 Apr 07:27 EST

Come over. Right now.

I’m here for you.

<3 T

Subject: FW: Last one, I swear

From: Ezra <e89898989@ymail.com>

To: Bea <b98989898@ymail.com>

Date: Sat 20 Apr 10:12 EST

I reached for him, Bea, and he was there. Terrence.

This simple thing that has never been an easy thing—this time it worked.

And I cried, because I don't think it's ever worked for me before. Not like this.

I cried because Mom was never there for me when I reached for her. Not really.

I cried because you're not here for me to reach for.

I cried because my father is dead, and I never got to reach for him.

I cried because you don't understand how deep the deep end goes until you're actually drowning.

I cried and it was almost okay, because I was crying in Terrence's arms. And this time he knew everything he needed to know, everything about me that needed to be held.

I cried because his presence allowed me to let myself cry.

I cried because at that moment, Bea, I was too exhausted to be angry, too defeated to lash out.

I cried because when I got to his house, his father didn't understand why I was there so early on a Saturday morning, and Terrence came right out and said, "He's my boyfriend, Dad. My *boyfriend.* I love him, and if that's a problem, we can talk about it later. Right now, he needs me, and there's no way I'm going to let you stand in the way of that."

I cried because I'd had no idea how much I had needed him to say that.

I cried because his father stepped aside, and his mother made me breakfast.

I cried because I am starting to realize that to love someone, to really love them deeply, is to want them to be family.

I let all these things crescendo within me. I let myself feel all of them at once. I felt the loss most of all. The loss of the home I never had. The loss of so much of my life until now. Loss should be a numbness. An emptiness. But it's not. It is the most painful part.

I wondered: Did Mom and Darren hurt us more by what they did or by what they didn't do? Which wounds us more—the hostile presence or the absent kindness?

I thought about all these things. I felt them all.

And then I took hold of not only Terrence, but everything else I have.

I told myself this is the restart, this is the first morning of something new.

I stopped crying.

I sat on my boyfriend's floor as he gathered my crumpled tissues and offered me another. He was joining me in the deep end, neither of us knowing what to say.

We've never been like this before. We've certainly left the shallows before, when he would vent about his father's conditional love and his mother's inability to persuade him out of it, or when I would share what I was willing to share about what was going on in our house. One night he asked me point-blank if the abuse had ever gotten more than yelling and the occasional shove and the even more occasional blow. And I told him that was the extent of it, and he said that was still more than too much. I didn't disagree, but we didn't go further than that, trying to figure out an escape plan. Not in the shallows, but treading water. Not the deep end, because I still thought I could find my footing if I stopped treading.

But now, in the deep end, I need him beside me because if I stop, if I tire, I will go under and not come back up. I may need him to carry me to shore, and he's letting me know he's strong enough to do it.

I'm still there. On his floor. In the deep end. Only now with his laptop, and him giving me a little space so I can write to you. He says I have to write to you. He says I have to understand the full situation.

I know he's right. I feel this could all go badly, me relying on him so much. But I also feel it would be stupid not to rely on someone who has always been reliable to me. I don't think I understood that until now. Not so clearly. The importance of reliability, because it's not something I've known much firsthand.

Okay, deep breath . . . this is what I want to say to you.

If London is who he says he is—and the only reason I'm thinking he might be is because I can't believe you would have given him my email address if he wasn't—I'm not sure I want to have anything to do with him. I feel bad that his father's dead. I feel bad that he's always wanted a brother. But I can't muster up any feelings other than those. The rest is my exhausted rage.

It makes it worse to know that our biological father was a good guy.

It makes it even worse to know that he's gone now, and that none of that goodness will ever come our way.

It makes it worst of all to have learned this from a stranger, not you.

I feel like my whole life I've been playing this game called *This* Is Not As Bad As *That.* I would tell myself that our life with Mom and Darren wasn't as bad as if they'd sexually abused us. Or hit us hard enough to break bones. Or kicked us out when they threatened to. Or prevented us from seeing Meemaw, the one person who actually tried to love us. It could always be worse. I've listed all the ways it could be worse. This Is Not As Bad As That.

Why didn't anyone ever tell me this was the wrong game to play? Why didn't I understand how broken my frame of reference was, and that I wasn't the person who'd broken it?

I've always felt the combustion inside of me, Bea. I always thought it was bright as the sun, and that if I let anyone see it, it would blind us all.

But I was wrong.

It wasn't a sun.

It's been an eclipse.

And now I'm feeling what happens when all the lies, all the games, all the denials are pulled away.

I understand why you left, Bea.

I completely understand why you left.

But we're still in the deep end, aren't we?

How the fuck do we get out of it now?

Ez

Subject: The Deep End
From: Bea <b98989898@ymail.com>
To: Ezra <e89898989@ymail.com>
Date: Sun 21 Apr 21:15 CST

Yes, Ez. It's true. We have a brother. A short, eager puppy of a fourteen-almost-fifteen-year-old brother named London who catfished me into leaving the only life I've ever known so that I could become a runaway and a dropout. You can't make this shit up.

I'm sorry I didn't tell you myself, but I couldn't. If I had, I might've gone back there and strangled that kid. Not that my life was ever going to be amazing, but the thought that I may have ruined what chance I had at it is pretty hard to stomach.

He looks like us, Ez.

This is what happened:

I met him at Forest Park, which is this giant city park that's home to the art museum, the zoo, the history museum, and the Turtle Playground, which is all these dinosaur-size turtle sculptures that you can climb on. It was a warm, blue-sky day, and it seemed like the entire city of St. Louis was out in it, meaning in the park. The playground alone was crawling with kids.

My first thought was *Maybe Dad doesn't remember that I'm eighteen now and too old to climb on turtle sculptures.* After all, the last time I saw him I'd only been walking for about a year.

I sat on the grass and waited. And then I thought better of it because what if he didn't see me down there on the grass? So I stood, and that seemed so formal, and I never know what to do with my arms, so I sat on the head of one of the turtles, legs swinging, trying to look all *la la la.* From that vantage point, I could see all sides. I wasn't sure which direction he'd come from.

Every time I saw a man of Dad's approximate age, my heart would do this leap and I'd be like *There he is* and go kind of breathless. And then the man would walk on by or head off in the other direction, and I would sink a little more, melting into the muddy brown concrete of the turtle's head.

Poor Bea.

Then—

At some point, this kid came walking up onto the shell of one of the other turtles. He stood there for a minute, shading his eyes, looking all around. I noticed him because he was wearing a bright red puffer vest even though it was like eighty degrees out. When he saw me, he jumped down off the shell and headed right for me.

I knew when I saw him that we had to be related. But even as he was walking toward me, even as it was dawning on me that this kid was tied to you and me in some way, I was still looking over his head for Dad.

"Hey," he said.

"Uh. Hey?"

He just stood there squinting up at me through these glasses, and the next thing he said? "Your hair's different. It used to be long. It's short now. And white."

"It's not white. It's blond."

"It looks white from down here. You're still pretty. Just different."

I said, "I'm meeting someone. Go away."

He said, "I know."

And that's when I knew Dad wasn't coming. That Dad, wherever he was, didn't have any idea I was here. My stomach did this flip and my bones went cold in spite of the heat.

He said, "Your dad is Jonathan Wooster. Jonathan Calvin Wooster."

"Jonathan Calvin Ahern."

"No. It's Wooster."

"Online you said it was Ahern."

"Because that's your last name. That's the last name you thought he had. I needed you to believe me."

"So you're telling me his last name was Wooster?"

"Yeah."

"Which means, what? My last name is really Wooster?"

"I guess?"

"Uh-uh. Hell no."

"I can prove it."

I'm not going to stand there arguing with a teenager who seems like he could argue for days. I say, "So?"

"So I'm his son."

"Whose son?" And I'm still looking around, just in case Dad is on his way, just beyond that tree or making his way down that path.

The kid said, "Jonathan Calvin Wooster." And he stuck out his hand and said, "I'm your brother."

I said, "No."

"Yes."

"No."

"Yes."

"I'm waiting for my dad."

"I know."

I said, "If you're really Jonathan Ahern—Wooster's—son, prove it." Even as my stomach is flipping and my bones are about to crack in two from frostbite.

And he holds up his phone and shows me all these photos of him and this man who looked a lot like Dad, or at least the Dad I sort of remember. And then he shows me his school ID, and there's his name—*London Wooster*—and a picture of him without his glasses, a little blurry, looking so much like me at fifteen that I actually thought it *was* me for a second.

And I go, "So you got his nose too. I'm sorry." And then I go, "*London?* Seriously?" And my heart is beating too fast because even though the name is different, I *know* it's him. This man. The one on his phone. Is our dad.

London goes, "Yeah. But they call me Lo. You can give me another nickname if you want."

"No thanks."

"I'm almost fifteen."

"Good for you. Where does the *Wooster* come from?"

"Your mom changed her last name after she left."

This sounds like Mom, but why should I believe this kid?

"What do you want, London Wooster?"

"Lo. To get to know you."

"Why?"

"Because our dad died last year and I'm an only child."

He said it just like that, Ez. *Our dad died last year.* So, so casual and matter-of-fact.

I said, "That's not my problem." But at this point I'm trying to breathe. I'm trying to concentrate on not falling off the head of this stupid dinosaur-size turtle and landing splat on the ground at his feet.

He said, "It's why you came here."

"To meet him, not you."

"But I'm here and he's not. So maybe you can get to know me. I'm sorry I lied to you, but I never thought you'd write me back. And then you did, and I couldn't believe it, and you actually thought I was him, and I wanted to talk to you some more, so I just didn't tell you it was me."

"You realize that's fucked up."

"Yeah."

"No, like seriously, certifiably fucked up."

"I didn't . . ."

"And I left my life to come here to see him. Not you."

"I'm sorry."

"I left Ez."

"Who's Ez?"

"Ezra. My brother."

"I have a brother?"

I said, "No."

"But—"

"No."

"But you just said—"

"No."

"Ezra? His name is Ezra?"

"No."

On and on, Ez, forever.

Until he said, "Maybe he could come here. . . ."

That's when I stood up, and I was a world taller than London Wooster because I was standing on the nose of that turtle. I said, "No. You need to stop. I'm not your sister. He's not your brother. Maybe technically, but that's it. We don't share a dad. How can we share a dad when Ezra and I never had one?" And maybe I was yelling it. Kids stopped playing. People were staring. I stared back. "He's not my brother," I yelled at them. "My brother's name is Ezra and he's back home. This"—I pointed at London—"IS NOT HIM." They stopped staring then, gathering up their children, hurrying away, looking at anything else but me.

London was crying by then, and I felt bad, but honestly, Ez, I felt worse for me. Because all I could think about was my list of questions.

Why did you leave us?

Was Mom always so shitty?

Are you as shitty as she says you are?

Do you know about Darren? Like, do you know how he treats your kids?

Would you treat us like that, if you were here?

What were you like when you were our age?

Did you even want *children?*

What are you most afraid of?

What's the one thing you've always wished you could do?

Which Avenger do you relate to most?

All these things I will never know the answers to because our father took the answers with him. And in that moment, standing there, I realized just how much I wanted to know the answers to those questions. Like, *needed* to know them. All my life, I haven't thought about Dad except to wonder why he hated us so much that he would not only leave us but leave us with our mother. And suddenly, for the past how many months, I'm thinking about him every day. And I realize how much I wanted to see him. And talk to him. And ask him every last one of those fucking questions.

And then I was crying, which made the world look like I was seeing it from behind one of those shower curtain liners that's gone foggy and water-splattered. Talk about being in the deep end. I never knew they made water that deep.

And then I climbed down and just walked away from this kid, our brother. But before I did, I said, "You were the one who did this. You need to be the one to tell Ez." And I grabbed his phone, typed in your email address, and left him there.

Subject: The Deeper End
From: Bea <b989898898@ymail.com>
To: Ezra <e898989898@ymail.com>
Date: Sun 21 Apr 22:47 CST

I walked away from St. Louis. Literally. Found Interstate 70 and walked until I was out of the city limits because I had to get as far away from there as I could, even if I had to do it on foot.

And then I started hitchhiking my way to Columbia. I don't know why, maybe because I'd heard of it, which is more than I can say for most Missouri towns. And maybe because the guy who gave me a ride was good-looking in a Golly Gee All-American kind of way and that's where he was going. His name is Patrick Aaron Robinson, called Patch by his friends, and he plays basketball at St. Louis University. Even though he looks like a good churchgoing boy—warm hazel eyes, easy smile—he was wearing a Sex Pistols T-shirt and there was a pinup-girl air freshener hanging from the rearview mirror of his truck. Old me would have taken one look at him and said keep on going, buddy. Because this guy is scary handsome. Remember Marcus Doyle, who was a class above me? Patrick Aaron Robinson is even better-looking. So old me would've been like, No way. I wouldn't even know what to say to a guy like this. But runaway/dropout me just climbed right into his truck.

At first he tried to talk to me, but when I didn't answer, he stopped. We rode most of the way without speaking, me in my head, thinking of how I'd just fucked up my life because of an almost-fifteen-year-old, and now this guy was going to kill me and dump my body in a field somewhere on the prairie because apparently I'm a terrible judge of character and serial killers sometimes look like regular churchgoing folk or Zac Efron (see *Extremely Wicked, Shockingly Evil and Vile*), and this guy was both. My brain was like, *Get out of the truck. Jump out right now, even if it's moving.* But my body kept sitting there.

At some point I said to him, "If you're going to kill me, you might as well do it now."

He looked at me like I'd lost my mind.

I said, "Go ahead. Seriously. It's better for me if you get it over with."

"Do you *want* me to kill you?" He was doing this half-smile thing, with dimples, like I was making some big fat joke.

"Not really."

"Then I won't."

Neither of us said anything for a minute, and then he goes, "You do know I was kidding, right? I'm not a murderer. I can't even catch a fish without releasing it. Something my dad finds extremely disappointing."

I said, "We're good."

"What's your name?"

"You don't need to know. I'm just here for the free transportation."

"You look like a Martha."

"Are you kidding me?"

"Yeah. You really do." *Flash flash dimple dimple.* "So if you don't want to tell me your actual name, that's what I'll call you."

You could tell he thought he was cute. Which he was, but that's not the point. I just rolled my eyes and stared out the window.

"So, Martha. Do you have some big life plan or are you seeing where the road takes you?"

He didn't mean anything by it, but something in me just snapped. Like all the things I was holding and carrying suddenly got too heavy, and one went plummeting to the floor, and then all of them went tumbling, and all at once my arms were empty and I'm holding nothing but air. It's not that I ever had big plans for myself, but all at once I didn't have any. Like in the moment I met London Wooster, anything even resembling a plan went away.

I started to cry. Again. Full-on ugly crying. Gasping and hiccupping and my entire self wet from all the tears.

He pulled the truck over to the side of the road, and this is when I thought it would happen. The killing. He turned off the engine. We sat there for two or three minutes, which felt more like two or three hours. I know it was two or three minutes because I was watching the clock on his dash.

Finally he goes, "If it were up to me, I'd be at KU—that's University of Kansas—with the rest of my friends. But my dad has other plans." Then he goes on about how he's more interested in criminal psychology than basketball, and it's just his dad and him, his mom died when he was small, and his dad doesn't see him, not really, even though he means well. And the entire time I'm sitting there crying into my hands, wondering if this is some sort of serial killer foreplay. Like he wants to confess all these things to me before he wraps his phone charger around my neck and boots my dead ass out onto the roadside.

Then he goes, "What's your excuse?"

I dropped my hands. I looked at him. "For what?"

"Running."

"Who says I'm running?" I dried my face as best I could with the backs of my hands.

He looked at me then, starting with my shoes, ending with my messy, wet face.

"You do."

I almost got out of the truck and took my chances on that long stretch of highway. But then I was like, I've got nothing to lose. And I've run this far, haven't I? And here I am on some Missouri highway, having left my brother—and this new other brother, deceitful shitbag that he is—and everyone I know, including Franco and Irene, behind. So I said, "You should try it. If you hate your life so much. Why don't you run away?"

He stared at me so long I thought, *This* is when he kills me.

And then he said, "You're right. Maybe I should. The thing is, Martha." He's got this soft, raspy voice that makes him sound like a phone sex operator. "The thing is, I'd rather run toward something than run from something. Does that make sense?"

I hiccupped. Nodded. Croaked out a "yes."

"I just haven't found the thing I want to run to yet."

He started the truck. We pulled back onto the highway and for the next mile I thought about this. *I just haven't found the thing I want to run to yet.*

I sat there thinking about all the running *from* I've been doing and how my running away was the first time I ever ran *to* something. Even if that something blew up in my face, I figure running toward is still better than running away.

And that got me thinking about stupid London Wooster with his stupid glasses and stupid face with Dad's stupid nose sitting right in the center of it. He was running to me. To us, Ez. He did it in a fucked-up, twisted way. But that doesn't change the fact that he ran to me. However he did it, maybe I should have listened. After all, family for you and me is in short supply and beggars can't be choosers, as they say. Maybe I shouldn't have given him your email. I'm sorry it didn't come from me. But in some ways, I didn't want to be the one to tell you. I felt like he owed you an explanation for why your sister left you behind. I felt like he owed us both that.

The farther away we got from St. Louis, the worse I felt. I couldn't get that kid out of my mind. So I asked Patch to turn the truck around and take me back. And at first he thought I was joking, but then he was like, "As long as you tell me your name."

"It's Martha," I said. "You were right."

I could tell he knew I was lying, but he said, "Okay, Martha." And turned the truck around.

I said, "I can hitch. Someone's probably waiting for you. Some college girl with perfect hair and a perfect life. You should go back to her. She misses you. She'll die without you. Even though she's smart and capable and probably on scholarship, even though she can afford to go to ten colleges at the same time if she wanted to. Her family has always been supportive and there for her in all the ways that count, and they believe in her, most of all. Anything for her. You don't want to keep her waiting. Felicity. That's her name. Don't keep Felicity waiting. No one keeps Felicity waiting."

And he goes, "No one's waiting for me. No one that matters. Especially not this Felicity you speak of. And hitching's dangerous." He flashed me that smile again. "Just tell me one thing. Is going back to St. Louis you running to something?"

"Maybe. Yes."

"That's good enough for me."

For a while, we don't say anything, and then he goes, "She sounds like a nightmare."

"Who?"

"This Felicity chick."

"*Chick* is demeaning. Unless you're an old person who doesn't know any better."

"Felicity then. She sounds like a lot."

"She is a lot. But a *good* a lot, as opposed to a *bad* a lot. I'm a bad a lot."

"Who says?"

"Everyone."

"Huh."

"Only I'm not."

"Not what?"

"A bad a lot. I actually think I'm pretty cool." And as I said it, I kind of believed it. I thought of standing on the turtle sculpture shouting at all the onlookers, all those people staring at me during the worst moment of my life like I was there for their entertainment, like I'd invited them to pull up a chair and watch the Bea Melts Down Show. I thought of them running away after I shouted at them and I couldn't help it, I laughed out loud in Patrick Aaron Robinson's truck.

He was looking at me, just like they looked at me, and I said, "You had to be there."

We rode in silence for a mile or two. I stared out at the ugly, boring landscape, wondering what it was like to grow up here. Wondering what our lives would have been like if we'd grown up here. I'm deep in my head, the way I get, and at some point Patch turned the music up, up, up, and I was suddenly aware that it's blasting and then I couldn't think about anything but the music. N.W.A.

I reached over and turned it down. "What?" I said.

"Oh good, you're still here. I said, I'm a bad a lot too."

"No you're not."

"I am."

I reached over again, this time to flip his visor down and point to the mirror. "No, you're not. Look at you."

He pretended to admire himself. "Take the wheel, Martha. I gotta get a good look at this." He let go of the steering wheel, and instinctively I grabbed it so that we didn't go careening off the road or slam into oncoming traffic, such as it was. He turned his head this way, that way, grinned at the mirror, winked.

Finally he sat back, arms folded, while I steered. "You think you know people because you've been hurt by them. I know what that's like. But don't pretend you know me." He flipped the visor up and took the wheel. And the air around us changed. He reached out one long arm, veins in his muscles twitching, and turned up the music again.

We didn't talk the rest of the trip. It took us an hour to get back to St. Louis, to the park, and by the time we got to the turtles London was gone. I didn't really expect him to be waiting for me in his puffer vest in the dark, but not seeing him there made me feel even worse.

I said, "He's gone." Even though it was obvious.

Patch said, "So let's look for him."

"You don't even know who I'm looking for."

"Doesn't matter. This is more interesting than anything I have to do right now. Felicity included."

"Fuck Felicity," I said.

He laughed. "Everly," he said.

"What?"

"Everly. The name of the girl I was going to see when you hijacked me."

"Everly?"

"Everly."

I rolled my eyes. "Everly. Felicity. Same thing. So are you sorry you're here? With me?"

"No." And I could hear the sincerity in his voice the way you and I can always tell if someone's telling us the truth or not. He had his hands in his jean pockets because the air had gotten cooler, and I thought, *He's someone who can stand around and know what to do with his arms.*

I said, "You're really handsome."

He laughed again. He said, "It's just my face." And he waved at it like *this old thing* and then slid his hand back into his pocket. "So do you know where he lives? The mystery person you were hoping to find here?"

"No, but I'll find him." I pulled out my phone and typed in *Jonathan Calvin Wooster,* and what do you know, just like that, an address pops up. After all these years of wondering about Dad, all we needed to do was type his name into a search engine, and there he is. You know, if we'd known his name.

I held up the phone to show him.

"That's him?"

"That's his dad. My dad, technically. He's apparently dead now."

"Okay. Sorry for your loss."

"Thanks. And, hey, thanks for the ride."

"Yeah. You're not getting rid of me that easy, Martha." He started walking ahead of me, back to the truck. When I didn't follow him, he turned around and said, "Well, come on. We can stay at SLU or we can go to my house and you can meet my very intimidating yet well-meaning dad."

"I've got places I can stay."

"Sure you do. Come on."

Which is why I'm writing this from the laptop of someone called Nando in a dorm room on the St. Louis University campus. This is the thing about life, Ez. You never know where it's going to take you.

Subject: The Deeper End—Part Two

From: Bea <b98989898@ymail.com>

To: Ezra <e89898989@ymail.com>

Date: Mon 22 Apr 01:28 CST

Okay, I'm back. You didn't know I was gone, which is the magic of these emails, but for the past two hours Patrick Aaron Robinson and I have been sitting on the roof of his dorm in two old lawn chairs, under a partly starlit sky, talking. Me, dressed in one of his basketball jerseys, which hung to my knees, while my filthy clothes got washed clean in the basement laundry room. The first thing I did was ask him about Everly.

"So what's her story?" I fixed my eyes on him. In case he decided to lie, I wanted to be able to see it.

"Everly's?"

"Yeah."

He took a drink. Stretched his long legs in front of him, crossed his ankles, shrugged. "I don't know. I kind of got distracted before I could find out."

"By me?" Even though I knew the answer.

He laughed. Nothing seems to get past him. "By you."

"How long have you been together?"

"We're not together. She goes to Mizzou. I met her here in

St. Louis at this dive bar called The Haunt. Last week. Me going to Columbia, that was going to be the first time we hung out."

All of a sudden, I felt like the stars were closing in. I don't know why, but I got mad. At him. At this girl in Columbia, Missouri, who probably has the nicest story you've ever heard, one without villains or sadness or people running away.

I said, "Don't let me stop you."

"Too late." And then he grinned at me. "If I'd really wanted to see Everly, I wouldn't have stopped to pick you up." Like that, the stars were back where they belonged, way up in the sky, and I could breathe.

"So what about you?" Now his eyes were fixed on me. "Who's waiting for you back home?"

"No one." But this felt like a lie, and out there on the roof, under the stars, I didn't want there to be any lies. "Actually Joe," I said. "Joe is waiting. But it's over—it's been over—for a long time. He knows, but . . ." My words drifted off. I didn't like Joe being there on that roof.

"But you're hard to shake."

I gave him a *haha fuck you* look, but he wasn't mocking me. He was smiling in this sweet, sexy, genuine way.

"I'm gonna need to keep my eye on you, Martha."

I couldn't help smiling then, and we sat like that for a few seconds, grinning at each other like two teenagers in a movie.

Then his eyes broke away from mine and stared out into the distance, where he pointed out his house, or at least the general direction of his house. He said he hadn't been back to see his dad since Christmas because they don't agree on his life. As in Patch is living the life his dad wants him to, but "It doesn't mean I have to be happy about it, and it doesn't mean he gets to ask me about it."

The whole conversation made me sad because at least his dad cares about him. I said, "At least he cares what happens to you."

"I know he does," Patch said. "But there's a difference between caring and listening. He doesn't listen."

I told him about Mom and Darren and how they don't care *or* listen, and then I told him how I just walked away from everything, including you.

He said, "I don't how much longer I can *not* walk away."

"So maybe you need to."

He shrugged.

"So do it," I said.

"It's complicated." And he sounded irritated, like he wanted me to shut up and leave it alone. But you know how I can get, Ez. Like a dog with a bone. I wasn't going to let it go.

"Or you could just keep complaining about it," I said, feeling kind of impatient and also irritated. I mean, I've never had much patience, Ez, but it's like now that I've been on my own and now that I've been through what I've been through I have even less. And saying this to him I felt a little older. And responsible in a way I'd never felt before. Because there I was giving this smart, gorgeous man—with the whole world laid out before him—advice like some wise old crone who had lived a hundred lives. And I wanted to shake him, to tell him to stop being one of those people who always talks and talks about the things he hates about his life without doing anything to change it. Sometimes people, even the smart ones, even the good ones, just can't see themselves.

As upside down as our lives might be right now, Ez? At least we're doing something to change it.

Anyway, I wanted to let you know what happened. I don't know where it all goes from here or where I go. But I do know that bright and early tomorrow morning—later this morning, I guess—the world's handsomest basketball player and I are going to Dad's old house to see about this boy who claims to be our brother.

Love,
Martha

p.s. He probably won't want to hear this from me, but tell Terrence thank you. I'm going to sleep better tonight knowing you're with him and that he knows what's happening and that, no matter what, no matter how deep the deep end gets, he has your back.

Subject: From Bea
From: Bea <b98989898@ymail.com>
To: franco@francositmarket.com
Date: Mon 22 Apr 1:50 CST

Dear Franco,

Please accept my apology. I'm sorry I haven't written to let you know I'm okay, but I haven't had computer access till now.

I came here to find my father. That is why I ran away from home. You may or may not have figured that part of it out. My "father" turned out to be a half brother I never knew I had. My actual father is dead. Old Bea would have just taken off and not said anything to you, even after all your hospitality. But I am trying to let Old Bea go. New Bea wants to say she's sorry to you and Irene.

I am trying to sort out some things. I know I left my belongings, such as they are, at your store. If I'm not back in a week or so, please feel free to throw them away.

Thank you again.

Your friend,
Bea

Subject: Late night wonderings

From: Bea <b989898989@ymail.com>

To: Ezra <e89898989@ymail.com>

Date: Mon 22 Apr 02:09 CST

When you're with Terrence, do you ever feel like you need to be on your best behavior and show him the very best Ezra? Like, do you feel this urge to sweep yourself under the rug or out onto the street and Pledge out all the dusty, cobwebby, rough, and broken spots so that he can't see them?

I never really felt that with Joe, but Patch is kind of intimidatingly good and kind and handsome and funny. And, as if all that wasn't enough, smart. For some reason, he likes talking to me—or else he's really good at pretending—but I wish I had a shinier, gleamier Bea right now who could take my place and sit beside him on the roof of his dorm and talk about the stars.

Subject: Sunday bloody Sunday

From: Ezra <e89898989@ymail.com>

To: Bea <b98989898@ymail.com>

Date: Mon 22 Apr 03:21 EST

So I started the day at church.

I know, I know—get your jaw off the ground. Stop checking the temperature in hell to see if it's dropped below zero. I was surprised too. But when Terrence's mom asked me if I'd come along with the family to church on Sunday morning, I knew it was a big deal. I could see on Terrence's face that it was a big deal. His mom was walking out on a limb she'd never tested before. I accepted the invitation.

The problem being: I don't exactly have the right clothes. And you know I'm hardly Terrence's size. But Terrence's mom is not deterred—no, she heads right to a closet I'd never even noticed before, and she takes out a suit she says belonged to Terrence's dad back in college.

So there I am, the white kid in the Black church, smelling of mothballs and with the cuffs of my pants constantly tucking under the backs of my shoes. And you know how people react? Like they're all happy to see me. Am I introduced as Terrence's "friend" rather than his boyfriend? You bet I am. Do I mind this? Not at all.

The service begins, and while I don't have any idea what to say or do, I know why I'm there. Not just because it feels so good to be welcomed, although there is that. No, the reason I'm at church this Sunday morning is because my father has died, and I didn't get to go to any funeral, and what I need right now is the space to have my own funeral in my head. There aren't any speeches in this funeral, because I don't know what to say. The casket is closed, because I don't know what he looks like. But all around me, there are prayers and songs, amens and hallelujahs. We're sitting in the back row of the funeral, Bea; nobody knows we're there. I see London in the front with his mom, sobbing. I see all of these other people reaching out to comfort them. I understand that this man I didn't know, this man who's died, has left memories inside all of these other people. As the funeral goes on, the memories are filling their heads. You and I strain to see them. We want to know just a little more. We want to feel we deserve to be there.

I start crying, there in the church—the real church, not the one in my mind. Not loud crying, but tears down my face that I try to wipe away quickly. Everyone is so busy with their *Jesus Jesus Jesus* that I don't think they'll notice. But Terrence's mom takes a tissue out of her purse and hands it to me. Then, when I'm done clearing my face of tears, she pats me on the hand. *It's going to be all right.* She doesn't have to say it; it's transmitted in that simple touch.

I say a prayer for London and his mom, because I know what

they're going through must be hard, and maybe they're the kind of people who believe in prayers.

After church, there's a lot of talking and catching up. Terrence asks his parents if we can walk home since the weather's so nice; I'm sure they understand that he's just looking for a way for us to get out of there, and they go along with it. It's only a half-hour walk, and we'll probably get back to the house before they do, in time for lunch (which they call dinner).

There's not much to say about the walk home—it's just a walk home on a nice day. As you can probably deduce, Terrence and I have spent a lot of time together this weekend, talking or taking a break from talking. There isn't much left to say, and that feels comfortable rather than awkward. He tells me some stories about the people I met in church, and I try to figure out who he's talking about. (He keeps referring to them by what they were wearing; I don't have the heart to tell him that while he notices details like that, I don't remember a single thing about what anybody wore.)

We're so busy talking that I don't notice Darren's car parked across the street from Terrence's house. Not until I hear Darren's voice calling my name, and I turn and see him there in the driver's seat, window rolled down.

"Ezra!" he calls out. "Get in this car *right now.*"

Mom is in the car with him, Bea. I can see her next to him, staring straight ahead.

"Now," Darren repeats.

I freeze.

Then, that warning: "Don't make me get out of this car."

I can't move.

I feel the tug of all the other times I've listened to him; it's practically instinct, that instantaneous measurement of demand vs. consequence, knowing it's always easier to give in to the demand than have it escalate into consequence. *Don't make me get out of this car. Don't make me say it again. Don't make me come over there. Don't make me take that thing out of your hands and throw it away. Don't make me hurt you. I don't want to hurt you, but I will.*

"Ezra," Terrence says, pulling at my arm. "Let's go inside."

The car door is opening. The car door is slamming. Darren is crossing the street.

Terrence is pulling harder. He is going to rip the sleeve of his father's suit.

Why can't I move?

Just go with him. Get in the car. You knew this was going to happen. You knew you couldn't stay here.

Terrence stops pulling on my sleeve. He's giving up on me. At that moment, I am sure he's giving up on me.

Walk away, Terrence, I think. *It's fine. I'll go.*

But instead of walking away, he steps between me and Darren.

"Get away from here!" Terrence yells. "This is our property."

Stop, I think. *It won't work.*

Darren laughs, stepping over the curb. "Sure. If this is your property, then he's his mother's property and I've come to retrieve it. It's time for him to apologize to her for everything he's done."

"Apologize?" I say.

He turns those angry eyes on me, full blast. "You are not going to hurt your mother any longer, do you understand? From now on, you are going to behave. Now stop all this shit and let's get your ass home."

What's the one word we were never allowed to use with Darren? Two letters, starts with an *N,* ends with an *O*? The trigger word. The unsafe word. The word guaranteed to piss him off more and make any punishment even worse.

I saw what happened when you used it. I heard what happened.

I also knew it never stopped anything. I knew he would storm right through it.

And if you want to know the truth, the despicably ugly truth, I might not have used it now, at this moment, if Terrence hadn't been there, if I hadn't been so embarrassed that Terrence was seeing me cut down to the core of my weakness. It was that mortification more than anything else that found a way to tell Darren no.

The second it was out in the air, he grabbed for me. Terrence tried to block him and got shoved aside. The rage, Bea—the pure rage. Darren tackled me right to the ground.

The jolt of hitting. Him right on top of me. Terrence crying out, then trying to pull him off. Me thinking *I am going to die* and also *I feel really bad about the suit.* More voices—neighbors running over. Shouting, "Get off him!" And then, miracle, Darren getting off me. Pulled back. Shrugging off Terrence and Mr. Anderson from next door. Mrs. Anderson yelling, "Police! I'm calling the police!" Maybe that's the word that gets through. I can't get up. He's yelling at them all now, saying this is his son, he can discipline his son however he wants. *You deserve this,* is what he's saying to me. Though now he won't look at me, still on the ground. A few more neighbors are coming out of their houses. "I'm going, I'm going," Darren spits out. I turn my head and look at the car.

Our mother, Bea.

Our mother.

Just.

Sits.

There.

Staring ahead through the windshield.

I'm over here, Mom.

I want to call it out, but I don't want Darren coming back.

Terrence reaches out to help me up. I touch the back of my head and Terrence says, "Oh shit," because there's blood on my fingers.

The car door slams again. The car makes a wide U-turn, and for a second I think he's going to run us over. But the car stays in the road, drives away.

Mrs. Anderson takes a look at the back of my head. Tells me

it doesn't look too bad, but I should stay there while she gets the first aid kit and some water.

I stay on the ground. Another neighbor, Mrs. Clemmons, says she got the whole thing on her phone, including the license plate. Terrence sits down next to me, holds my hand. The neighbors notice and don't comment. Instead Mr. Anderson introduces himself, and so does Mrs. Clemmons.

Mrs. Anderson is cleaning off the wound ("Just a cut," she assures me) and bandaging me when Terrence's parents pull up.

There are a lot of things to explain, and I don't hold back.

I explain them all.

They call the police. They remind the police what Darren did in the movie theater. They ask about a restraining order. The police say they'll warn him to stay away, and explain the steps for getting a restraining order. Nobody talks about social services, foster care, all of those things I'm afraid of. They ask about you and I make sure to say you're eighteen, that we're in touch, and that you're fine. Terrence's family also makes it sound like I'm already living here, like they've already taken care of it.

I'm not telling you all this to distress you. I'm fine. It sucked seeing him again—but it also helped me to know that the more people hear my story, the more I find out they're on my side, not his. I'm still scared, but I don't feel out of my mind for feeling scared. Not nearly as much as I did before.

Terrence's mom was ready to call our mom and give her a

good tongue-lashing—I've honestly never seen the woman so angry. But I surprised myself by telling her, no, that was something I had to do. Not right now. But soon. I keep thinking of her sitting in that car, staring as if the car was moving forward, and I know that I can't just give her my silence. No. There will come a time, soon, when I am going to have to throw my words at her. Because *that,* more than any silence, is what she should be carrying with her right now.

Just not tonight. It's late. Terrence says he's not waiting up for me, but I know he is. All these things happen . . . and still there's school tomorrow.

But, hey, you know that because you're in a dorm room. What's that look like, Bea—college? We should both try it sometime, no?

First things first, though. You find out what you can about our father.

And I—well, I'm going to figure out what I need to say to our mother. Once and for all. Suggestions welcome.

Ez

PS—Tell London I say hi. Because why the hell not, right?

Subject: #fuckdarren

From: Bea <b989898989@ymail.com>

To: Ezra <e89898989@ymail.com>

Date: Mon 22 Apr 07:36 CST

Holy shit, Ez.

Holy. Shit.

So of course I immediately go online to find out if Darren's been locked up, but if there's anything out there about evil stepfather + unfit mother + fight with teenage son of unfit mother in front of teenage son's boyfriend and neighbors, I don't see it.

I tell Patch about my badass little brother because, as miserable and god-awful as I know that was, I'm really, really proud of you, and he's the one who lets me know this is an even bigger deal than Darren trying to bully you/drag you into the car. This goes so far beyond our usual. My mind doesn't fully grasp this at first because I'm so used to keeping quiet about Darren and Mom and all the sordid things that happen behind closed doors over at good old 885 Hidden Valley Circle, so my first reaction is HOLY SHIT, MY BROTHER IS A BADASS, AND IF I *EVER* SEE DARREN AGAIN, I WILL KICK HIM IN THE FACE SO HARD HE'S GOING TO BE CHEWING WITH HIS NOSE.

Don't get me started on our mother.

But as I'm telling him, Patch sits up, all serious, and starts shaking his beautiful head. "Jesus, Martha," he says with a kind of whoosh sound, as if he's been holding his breath till just this moment. "He's really lucky that he has a place to stay."

Me: "Yeah." But now I'm worrying about Terrence and his parents and how long their hospitality will actually last.

"But," he goes, "and I didn't think about this—the police might tell your mom her husband has to leave, and then it's all okay. Ezra could go back home if he wants to." He is also a pretty positive person, something that might get on my nerves if he wasn't so cool and self-aware.

Now, you and I both know what the answer *should* be if the police suddenly tell Mom she has to choose between you and Darren. It would *have* to be you, right? Her son? I mean, what kind of mother steals her own kids from their father and then ditches them for her shitbag new husband?

Maybe the kind of mother who pretends that the new husband isn't grabbing her son and trying to force him into a car. Where she sits. Staring out the window. As if nothing is happening.

No.

No.

Fuck her.

Fuck them both, Ez.

I'm going to send this now and hopefully you write me back right away.

I'm sorry I'm not there.

I'm sorry I left you.

I'm sorry.

I'm sorry.

I'm sorry.

Love,

Bea

Subject: From Franco
From: franco@francositmarket.com
To: Bea <b98989898@ymail.com>
Date: Mon 22 Apr 08:02 CST

Bea,

Thank you for letting us know where you are. You take care of yourself. Your things are here. We aren't going to throw them away.

Your friend,
Franco

Subject: SLU (my day Part One)

From: Bea <b989989898@ymail.com>

To: Ezra <e89898989@ymail.com>

Date: Mon 22 Apr 22:13 CST

I'm not exactly sure how to start this letter. We both know I went to see our brother today. The only thing I can do is describe it.

But first.

Patch and I leave campus around 10 am, after his Intro to Criminal Psychology class. To save time, I go with him. No one knows I'm there because there are probably two hundred students in that lecture hall. The professor is young, maybe late thirties, and they call her Dr. Naomi, her first name. That's how hip she is. Anyway, I sit by Patch, concentrating on the smell of his soap, the nearness of him, so that I can distract myself from the following two things: A) The fact that my younger brother (you) has just gone through a major public battle with our mother's asshole lover; and B) The fact that I will be spending this day with my surprise *younger* younger brother (London) and his mom (who isn't our mom) at their house, which used to be the house of our recently deceased father.

So I'm breathing in Patch and breathing him out, and

completely blanking out on Dr. Naomi's lecture. Until she starts talking about nature vs. nurture and the impact on criminals. *Are they born bad? Are their criminal tendencies a product of genes? That's debatable. Or is it something in their upbringing, in their home environment, societal environment, parental experience—is that what creates them?* On and on.

I don't realize my hand is in the air until Patch nudges me in the ribs. His gaze follows my arm upward. My gaze follows his, up, up, up to my hand, raised for all to see. I drop it back down, but too late. Dr. Naomi says, "Yes?"

She says it in such a friendly way. So welcoming and non-judgmental. Which is why I open my mouth and say, "What if it's a combination? What if they're born with bad tendencies, what if we all are, but those tendencies are nurtured by their specific environments? What if their genetic makeup isn't any more screwed up than anyone else's, just the normal amount, but they're told over and over and over again that their only choice is to be bad?"

Because—what's this? I'm actually beginning to believe that you and I aren't the problem here, Ez, no matter what Mom and Darren say. Funny how you can believe things about yourself if someone tells you enough. *They* are the problem.

Dr. Naomi seems to appreciate this comment, and she gives examples of those who've been brainwashed into crime—people like cult followers and the Manson girls. I sit there thinking about the Manson girls and feeling better about myself—as shitty as Mom and Darren are, I would never murder anyone or brand a swastika on my forehead. And then, like that, the class is over.

"Good work today," Dr. Naomi says to me on our way out. You can tell she's searching for my name.

"Martha," I say.

"Martha," she repeats. "I look forward to more from you."

And this is the first time in my life anyone has ever said this. Like that, I freeze, unable to move, until Patch lays his hands on my shoulders and steers me out of the room.

College. I think about it all the way to London's house. I've never thought about college. I mean, I used to, about a hundred years ago when I was little. Back when I was tutoring Celia What's-her-name and reading books even Mom and Darren (you know, if they actually read) couldn't comprehend. But once I hit high school, I learned it just wasn't an option. There wasn't the money or the expectation. I still thought about it now and then, but we both know thinking about it and having it be an actual possibility are two different things. If it had been possible, I would have stayed and graduated with Joe and Sloane and the rest of my class, but that never seemed to matter.

College.

I'm picturing myself—another version of me, more put together, a little less runaway, a little more runway—walking across campus, sitting in lecture halls, raising my hand, getting into debates with professors and other students. I imagine my dorm room, decorated in bright colors, maybe Andy Warhol prints.

I'll dress like Edie Sedgwick, all smoky eyes and mod skirts and boots, maybe an ironic beret. I'll wave to everyone and go to the occasional party, but no one except Patch and my close-knit circle of friends will know me, really know me. Everyone else will buzz about how smart I am, though. How mysterious. How they've heard I overcame my *circumstances* to be here.

I envision myself in a cap and gown, walking across the stage, you in the audience with Terrence and maybe London, and Patch, smiling his proud, too-handsome smile. I'll give a speech about forgiveness and believing in yourself, and how if I can do it, anyone can. There will be tears from the audience, tears from me, and I'll walk off that stage knowing in my heart that I can do anything.

It's a beautiful daydream for a Manson girl, isn't it?

Love,
Bea

Subject: London Wooster (my day Part Two)

From: Bea <b98989898@ymail.com>

To: Ezra <e89898989@ymail.com>

Date: Mon 22 Apr 23:02 CST

Part Two

The Home of London Wooster

Patch drives me across St. Louis, giving me a pep talk. For once, I want to hear it. I could use some positive words. My own head is always such a negative, self-doubting place, although maybe a little less than it used to be. He talks and I listen.

"No matter what happens, this doesn't change who you are. It doesn't change the fact that you, Martha, are brilliant and amazing, that your smile—when you use it—could light up the dark Missouri sky. That your brain works in fascinating, dangerous ways. That you are braver than you think. That you are a human firework, all electricity and bright, bright colors. That you will always have your brother Ezra, no matter how far from home you wander, no matter how many half brothers or sisters pop up along the way."

Before I can start picturing a slew of little Londons, dressed in matching red puffer vests, showing up one by one by one, Patch says, "Hey, Martha. You got this."

"What about you?" I say.

"What about me?"

"You should tell your dad you've got your own dreams."

He waves his hand at this. Stares out the windshield at the road. "We're talking about you," he says in a minute.

"We're always talking about me," I say, and there's an edge to my voice, even though you know me, Ez. I've always liked it when things are about me.

"You're just a lot more interesting. And besides, my problems have been there for a while. No need to address them right now." He reaches for the radio, cranks it up, and starts singing loudly to some old Prince song. It's horrible, and I laugh, and then he's laughing and we're good. I sing the rest of the way at the top of my lungs, and I can't remember when I last did this—took up this much space, made this much noise, and didn't worry about it. His voice joins mine and then he reaches for my hand and I let him take it. I used to hate holding hands with Joe. Something about it felt clingy and suffocating. But sometimes it's good to feel human skin other than your own.

I keep an eye on the GPS. I can see the miles counting down until we're two miles away. *One mile away. Half a mile away. A quarter of a mile. Two blocks. Seven hundred feet.*

We drive through a respectable upper-middle-class neighborhood. Manicured trees, two- and three-story homes, some with porches, some without. Not McMansions, but older houses, houses with character. Lots of SUVs parked in driveways.

Five hundred feet. Four hundred feet. Three hundred feet. Two hundred feet. And suddenly there it is—the only house like it on the street, maybe in the entire neighborhood. All angles and multiple stories. Very modern, but, like, modern in a beautiful way. Like a Picasso.

The front door opens before I get out of the car, before Patch can finish telling me to call him when I'm done, no matter what time, and he'll come back to get me. Before he makes me repeat (for the tenth time) his phone number so that I can call him since I still don't have a phone of my own to program his number into. London stands on the step, Spider-Man shirt bagging around him, and waves.

For one second, I think about telling Patch to drive away, to get us the hell out of here. To tell him I won't step out of this truck until he faces his own dad and stands up for himself, for his life, the way I'm trying to do.

But then he says again, "You got this, Martha." And I don't want to disappoint him, and I don't want to disappoint London, who stands grinning and waving like we're in some giant crowd and he's worried I don't see him.

So I close the door to the truck, Patch on one side, me on the other, and walk up the neat stone path. London holds out his hand to shake mine, and instead of telling him, *You're such a weird almost-fifteen-year-old,* I shake his hand and follow him inside.

I want to describe every detail to you, Ez, but this is already long and I haven't even gotten in the house, and there is so much to say. The house is one that Dad designed. He wasn't an architect, but London says he could draw, and when he was younger he wanted to study architecture. As modern as the house is, it feels warm and homey inside. Kind of like a magazine, but without everything too matching. Open and airy, but lived-in. Lots of light. Lots of art on the walls. Photographs our dad took, mostly black-and-white, of trees and skies and horizons. Lots of open spaces. London shows me Dad's camera, and I hold it in my hands and try to imagine this man I didn't know carrying it around and capturing moments. I try not to think of all the moments we lost.

Before London can give me the whole tour, a woman appears. She is smiling and pretty. Big dark eyes, red lips, auburn hair that waves around her forehead and cheeks. She shakes it out of the way. It hits exactly at her shoulders. She says, "I'm London's mom. Amelia. You must be Bea." She's Southern, which somehow seals the deal. At first glance, she is perfect and the complete opposite of our mother.

And then she hugs me as if it's the most natural thing in the world. Hugs. Me. The oldest child of her dead husband. A complete stranger who's bound to be a disruption in her life. She wraps her arms around me, slim yet strong, and gives the kind of mom hug I've only seen on television or in the movies. She smells like honey and flowers—roses, maybe—and I breathe her in.

She pulls away too soon and offers me something to drink, and London and I finish the tour, which ends in his room. It's no bigger than yours or mine. Maybe even a little smaller. But it's filled with all his favorite things. He shows them to me one by one—the pillow he once used for the tooth fairy, the one with the little pocket sewn in front; his Avengers action figures; the Spider-Man costume he wore for Halloween when he was ten; his old Nerf guns; his books; the last photo Dad took of him. On and on and on until I feel the walls closing in.

I have to get out of that small, happy room. He's in the middle of a sentence, of showing me something, when I turn and walk back toward the stairs. Our brother follows me, book in his hand, and we go back to the living room, where Amelia has set two glasses of what looks like iced tea on the glass coffee table. I drink mine down even though my mouth puckers from all the lemon and sugar, and sit on the long, sunken couch, a dark green, and stare out at the view. There is a lake or a pond, some sort of body of water. London drops down next to me and says, "That old creek. Dad used to joke that we had waterfront property."

Amelia comes in then and sits, and there we are. The three of us, four counting Mustache the dog. London says to her, "Remember that? How Dad used to say we lived on the water?"

"I do."

She sees my empty glass, hops up again, and rushes out to fill it. My mouth is coated with the syrupy, too-sweet taste of it, but I don't stop her because she's being so nice.

I say to London, "Is she always like that?"

"Like what?"

"Nice like that?"

He shrugs. "Pretty much."

London stares at me. I stare at him. I say, "I'm sorry about the other day."

"It's okay. It's my fault. I tricked you. I shouldn't have pretended to be Dad. I wouldn't have done that if I'd known you would leave home and school and Ezra to come here."

"Yeah, you shouldn't have done that." And I can see myself—shaggy bleached hair, clean but rumpled T-shirt and jeans, frown on my face. What a disappointment I must be as a long-lost sister. I add, "But I'm glad I know about Dad." And I don't just say it because I feel I owe him some speck of kindness. I say it because it's true.

He smiles and I let myself smile too. *See? Not so hard. You just let your face relax and out it comes.*

Amelia appears, setting a full glass of tea down in front of me, then sits across from me on the edge of a chair, leaning forward, arms on knees.

I don't know what to say, so I wave my hand at the books stacked on a nearby shelf. Shiny collector's editions of James Joyce, Herman Wouk, Zora Neale Hurston. "I've read all of those," I say. Which is true.

Amelia's eyebrows shoot up and she follows my gaze to the

books. "I didn't think anyone anywhere had ever made it through Joyce." She laughs.

"I have." It sounds flat and humorless, which is exactly the way I feel, like some sort of Bea paper doll, propped on this couch, hoping a strong wind doesn't come through and blow me away.

"Well, isn't that something?" she says, all Southern good manners. She nods at London. "Has he apologized yet?" she asks.

"Yes."

"Good." She's smiling. Her tone is friendly but mom-ish. "My turn. I want to say I'm sorry on his behalf." And I'm not sure if she means London or our father. "My son understands what he's done." Oh, okay. London, not our dad.

And then we sit and talk, like old friends. Amelia Wooster is warm and lovely with her singsong voice. We make polite chit-chat, something I've never been good at, and finally she says, "I'm sure you have questions." And then sits there waiting for me to ask them.

I completely forget my list of Dad questions, the one I've been keeping all my life. Instead I ask the first thing that pops into my mind. "Is it true he cheated on our mom with you?"

She doesn't blink. Doesn't hesitate, as if she knew I was going to ask it. "Yes. Technically."

"Can I ask—I mean—what happened exactly? Not details, of course, but . . ." I trail off.

"Well." She glances at London, and I wonder if I should be asking her this in private, not in front of her child.

"Sorry—"

"It's okay. So, Bea. No excuses, but toward the end it wasn't a happy marriage. And your dad and I met, and . . . well. We just knew."

"Knew what?"

"That we were meant to be together." She gives a helpless little laugh like *Oh, fate. What can you do?*

And I can tell she believes these words, but in my opinion this is not something you say to your dead husband's estranged daughter, especially when you're responsible for breaking up his marriage to said estranged daughter's mother, horrible though she may be.

"It takes two, of course. I know that. He knew that. So I owe you an apology as well, Bea. I'm sorry for my part in this. Truly. Deeply. Sorry."

It's so sincere, it catches me off guard. I feel an unfamiliar burning at the back of my eyelids. At first I think it's pink eye or some sort of bizarre infection that's sprung up out of nowhere, maybe due to all the expensive, filtered air. But then I realize it's the tears I'm holding in.

"Thank you," I say. But it's hard to get the words out because I'm feeling too many things at once. Amelia is genuinely nice. She is a nice person. My mother is not a nice person. My father may or may not have been a nice person. But for the first time in my life I feel protective of my mom. The same mom who hasn't even phoned the police to tell them I'm missing. The same mom who once told me she never expected anything of Ez or me, but especially me, because we were too difficult and too damaged. Those were the exact words she used. *Difficult. Damaged.*

London fidgets. He's a young almost-fifteen in a lot of ways. An old almost-fifteen in others. A childish little old man. He wants to go play, to show me the creek, to show me the basement family room and the loft on the top floor, but I have more questions. I want to know if Amelia ever met our mother, if our dad and mom tried to work it out or if he was done once he met his nice, so nice, soon-to-be second wife. Did he ever find us? Did he try, like really try? What kind of dad was he? Is it true he didn't know about Ezra?

My questions spill out onto the green couch, onto the glass coffee table, onto the magazines splayed out there—*Architectural Digest, The New Yorker, Garden & Gun, Vanity Fair*—onto the geometric-print rug.

Amelia says, "I never met her. Anne. No. I've spoken to her on the phone, but never met her."

"You spoke to her?"

"Once. She called the house after we were married to tell him you had a new father and to stop looking for you."

"Darren. Her husband. He's an asshole. Not a father."

"I'm sorry. Are they still together?"

"Unfortunately. Although as far as I know he's in jail now. You know, if there is a God."

Her eyes go a little wide. Then she smooths herself back in place, all composure and red lips, and shiny, shiny hair. "Your mom and dad were married for six years. They both called it a mistake, but said you were *not* part of that mistake. You were very much wanted."

"That's comforting." It comes out sarcastic, which it is.

"He came close to finding you once. He'd hired a detective and he was able to track her down. That was when she called, before the detective even filed a report. She said she would take you away, far away, if he ever tried to find you again. And that she would make sure you never went in search of him. So. Yes. He tried. He lost sleep over it. He never was a good sleeper to begin with. He used to lie awake and toss and turn. He said he never could shut off his brain."

Like me, I think.

"Did he stop looking then? After she called?"

"Yes."

"Why?"

She shifts, and she's uncomfortable, and something about that makes me feel like I'm in charge here. I take a long drink of the too-sweet tea and set the glass down beside the coaster. She frowns at it.

"Why did he stop looking?"

At this point I'm on a roll and I can only go forward, not back, toward everything I need to know.

"I think he just knew he couldn't win against her . . . ," she says to the table, to the ring of condensation that's growing there. "But he was our dad. He had just as much right to us as she did."

Her eyes are on mine again. "It just . . . I don't know how to explain it, except that he felt it would be easier for everyone. . . ."

"That makes sense. Because my life has been really easy. I mean, I can't tell you how easy it's been."

Amelia and London are staring at me, and I wonder for a second if they're afraid of me—this angry stranger coming into their house and losing her shit. I have this urge to throw something just to make them jump. I wonder if I could lift the coffee table and launch it through the floor-to-ceiling windows.

"So basically," I say, "let me get this straight. He gave up looking for his kids because he'd found a new wife." She opens her mouth. Closes it. "And Ezra?" I say.

A slight pause. Then: "He didn't know about Ezra."

"He didn't know?" My voice is too loud in this beautiful, pristine space. It goes smashing into the white walls and the black-and-white framed photos and the simple but tasteful furniture, and I see both Amelia and London flinch.

"Not at first. Not for a while."

"I see." I imagine throwing the chair, the books, the framed black-and-white photos one by one by one into the creek.

"What kind of dad was he?" I turn on London now. His owl eyes are wide and staring. He looks scared shitless, cat got his tongue, like he's just now realizing how real this all is. I repeat the question.

"He was a good dad . . . ," Amelia begins.

"I'm not asking you. I'm asking him." I stare unblinking at London.

Those owl eyes turn from her to me. "He was a good dad. He was nice. He listened. He was funny—"

"In a kind of dry way," Amelia interjects, leaning over, setting my glass on its coaster and wiping the table with her napkin.

"Yeah," London says. They both chuckle, as if remembering something specific, and in that moment I hate them both for every shared moment, every shared memory of our father. "Sometimes I didn't get it, but Mum says I'm more literal."

"Very literal," she says, but not in a mean way.

"Mum?" I blink at him.

"My name *is* London." He blinks back at me like it's all so obvious.

"Got it." Even though I don't.

London goes on, "Dad made things fun. Math. Reading. Homework. He turned them into adventures sometimes. He hated to be inside. He loved being out in the sun. We rode bikes and we would race each other. He always let me win, even though he was faster. He collected lucky pennies and then whenever we went somewhere, he would carry them in his pocket and leave them for people to find. He was good with animals."

He keeps going, but honestly that's all I hear, Ez. It's like my ears have heard all they can for the day, and they're done. Everything else is just a mumble of words from somewhere far away. I watch London's lips move, underneath our dad's nose, and I know he's talking, but it's garbled, like it's being transmitted over a walkie-talkie all the way from Kansas.

At some point, he finishes, and he and Amelia sit looking at me like it's my turn. Suddenly I can't think of what to say. *Good for you. He sounds like a helluva guy. He sounds like a great dad. He sounds like a great husband. He sounds like a great human being. I'm so glad you had this life that Ez and I should have had, or at least been part of in some small way.*

They are waiting and I am being rude by not saying anything. I know this much about manners. I search my brain for words that make sense, for words that won't sound desperate and sad, that won't make them feel sorrier for me than they already do.

Finally I hear myself say, "Which Avenger did he relate to most?"

Amelia and London look at each other. It's a stupid question and I can feel them thinking how stupid it is—they're probably like *sweet Jesus, where did she come from?*—and my cheeks go red-hot.

But then, at the same exact time, they say, "Bruce Banner."

"Not the Hulk," Amelia adds. "The actual man."

And it's such a little thing, but suddenly I'm crying, not like in the car with Patch. Long, rolling tears, one at a time, the kind that burn your skin.

All my life, I've been furious with our dad. I've hated him and cursed him for leaving us with Mom and been so fucking angry that I wanted to kill him if I ever saw him again. And now, sitting in his living room, in the house he designed for his other family, I'm filled with this sick, guilty feeling, like I'd actually murdered someone. As if all this time, I'd betrayed him. Going from the emptiness and anger I've carried around with me like extra limbs, as much a part of me as my legs or arms, to a hollowed-out feeling of loss because this man actually wanted me. At least for a while.

All at once, Amelia is beside me, arms around me, rocking me a little. This woman who was married to our dad for years, who maybe knew him better than anyone. And we'll never know him, Ez. We will *never know him.*

I start crying harder, and then London is on my other side, taking my hand in his, short, stubby fingers with these perfectly smooth, unchewed nails. I stare at his nails thinking how if I'd grown up here with our father and Amelia and London and you, I never would have chewed my nails. I wouldn't have had any reason to.

And then I push them both away and stand up, snotty, face soaked, wobbly from crying so much. They want me to stay.

Amelia is cooking a roast for dinner and London wants me to meet his friends. He can call them and they can be over here in five minutes because Wormy and The Meg, or whatever their names are, they both live close by.

"No," I say.

Because suddenly I have to get out of there. I could stay, but what would be the point? This isn't my house and this isn't my family, no matter how nice and *we're-so-glad-to-have-you-here-Bea* they are. It's too lovely. Too perfect. And it's not real. At least it's not real to me. My heart feels like it's going to shatter into a million pieces. If you're used to people being shitty, it's hard to accept niceness. Your instinct is to fuck it up. And run the hell away.

I don't even ask if I can call my friend to come get me. I make an excuse about having to meet someone, and thank them for everything, and try to carry the glass into the kitchen, but Amelia takes it from me.

London follows me to the door. "When are you coming back? My birthday's next week and I'm having a party. You can meet everyone and they can meet you."

Amelia clears her throat. She knows I'm not coming back because this is how perceptive and in tune our father's second wife is. She is a kind, sensitive, nice, nice person who sees people clearly. "We're just grateful to have this time with you, Bea. You're always welcome here, isn't she, Lo? But we know you have places you need to be."

Even though I don't. I don't have anywhere I need to be. No one is counting on me. No one is waiting for me. No one is looking for me. The only man who ever bothered looking for me is gone.

I bolt out the door, and Patch is there in his truck, as if he never left. The sight of him makes me start to cry again. *Why is everyone being so nice to me?*

I'm halfway across the lawn when I hear my name. It's Amelia, running after me, carrying a shoe box. She says, "I wanted you to have these." And hands the box to me. Nike. Men's. Size 12. *Dad's.*

"What is it?" I say.

"Letters. Every letter your dad wrote your mom. I thought you should have them. He'd want you to have them."

"Thank you." And then, even though I don't want to, I hug her, and it doesn't feel unnatural but like the only thing to do. Then I climb into Patch's truck, box on my lap, and we drive away. I don't look back.

I want to write more, but that's all I've got in me, Ez.

I feel pretty raw and sad and like I need to crawl into the corner and pull my shirt up over my head.

I wish you were here. I wish I was there. I want to go home, but not our home.

When I look at London Wooster and his life, I think no wonder he turned out to be a sweet (though odd) boy. He has the freedom to be weird and funny and wear a red puffer vest in spring because he's never once had to worry about disappointing anyone. He has that self-assurance that comes with knowing you are loved. We've never had that except with each other. I hope you've always felt that from me. I've always felt it from you.

Love,
Your sister,
Bea

Subject: Allies

From: Ezra <e89898989@ymail.com>

To: Bea <b98989898@ymail.com>

Date: Tues 23 Apr 00:35 EST

Terrence is asleep, so I can take my time here. My head is spinning, but maybe if I get some words out, it won't spin quite as much.

First up, it feels like you traveled into the Alternate Universe of Dad. That's the only way I can think of it, as this thing that's run parallel to my life but will never connect. I know I should feel something, reading about it. But I don't. My life isn't there. My life is here. I'm sure it would be different if he was alive and there was a chance of a new start. But that's not what we're looking at, is it?

But who am I kidding? Something this sharp is bound to sink in, right? Wiping us off our father's map? Who the hell is our mother, Bea?

I'm starting to think there's only one way to find out. Go straight to the source.

And at the same time, I'm also realizing how much we learned about our own family by comparison, which a lot of the time was the same thing as omission. Like that first time in elementary school when someone told me about the book they were reading with their mom or dad before they went to bed, and I thought, Oh, is that a thing parents do? Or when you'd go to a birthday party and the parents wouldn't be acting like it was some contractual obligation to be there. And now that I'm at Terrence's house, I can see all these ways that he's included in the conversations, in a way we were never included. I don't think Mom and Darren ever cared very much what we said, as long as what we said followed whatever rules they'd laid down. The quieter we were, the more they liked us. No, that feels like too much. Did they ever really like us? So I'll say it like this: The quieter we were, the more they didn't seem to mind that we were there.

All of which is I guess my way of saying that you going to see the Alternate Universe of Dad is the most extreme game of compare/contrast yet.

Maybe the mistake was thinking we were one family in our house. What if we were really two families? Mom and Darren in one, and you and me in another. Or Mom and Darren in one, and then outside of that, or overlapping a little, the four of us. It just happened that the Mom-and-Darren family was always the more important one. We were just too young to see it. Or too scared. I don't know.

I also have to say this (then I'm going to bed).

I guess I'm glad our dad tried to write to us.

But at the same time, I think I'm always going to feel he could've tried a little harder than that.

Subject: Alternate Universe of Bea
From: Bea <b989898898@ymail.com>
To: Ezra <e89898989@ymail.com>
Date: Tues 23 Apr 09:02 CST

I am in Patch's room. He has class and his roommate has class, and I am here, sitting on the floor, back against his bed, the contents of that shoe box spread out before me. I'm pretending this is my room, with the vintage whiskey posters tacked to the walls and the smell of boy everywhere. I imagine my life as a college student. Hanging out in the dorm between classes, going to parties, reading every book in the library, actually checking them out and taking them back to my room because I'd have my own student ID, one that would entitle me to books and meals in the cafeteria. Getting into passionate, life-altering debates in class, and the other students—my fellow students—being like, "That's just Bea. There she goes again." And maybe even saying, "Bea Ahern knows her shit," with a huge degree of awe. I imagine interning for professors—maybe something to do with publishing or writing. Definitely something to do with reading. I imagine venturing out into the world with a college degree, able to go anywhere and do anything I want.

Someone pounds on the door and yells, "You in there, bro?"

I'm so deep in my fictitious college life that I jump about ten feet. I yell back, "No!" in the deepest, loudest voice I can muster. They stand there a minute—I can see the shadow of feet under the door—but eventually they go away.

There are sixteen letters from Dad.

Sixteen.

I expected more. Do we think there should be more? I can't decide. How many is enough in this situation? Over a span of, what, fourteen or fifteen years?

The first letter goes back to the year you were born, five months after Mom left him. You hadn't arrived yet. You still had a month to go. Dad asks our mother to come home. He says:

We can work this out. Our daughter, not us. Let's not fuck her up the way our parents fucked us up. Please come back and we can talk about this, or I can meet you somewhere.

The letter came back as "undeliverable." None of the others were mailed.

Here's another:

You were the one who said we never should have gotten married. For a long time, I didn't want to believe you, but guess what, you were right. You were right, Anne. Is that what you need to hear? I'm sorry I didn't believe you and that I held out hope that our marriage could actually be a real and happy union. By the time I recognized that, I met Amelia and you know what happens afterward. If it makes you feel better to call me a shit heel and tell everyone I wronged you, go ahead.

Bottom line is I'm not interested in rehashing us. I just want you to bring my daughter back. I'm sorry for what I said. She could never be in the way. Not of us, not of me, not of our life. I didn't mean it, not even as I was saying it.

She could never be in the way.

Which implies that he must have, at some point, told her I was in the way.

If we were ever wondering if our parents were the great American love story, Ez, this confirms that they weren't. More like American Horror Story. But didn't you hope they might have loved each other for at least a little while?

Subject: Alternate Universe of Bea (two)
From: Bea <b989898898@ymail.com>
To: Ezra <e89898989@ymail.com>
Date: Tues 23 Apr 09:48 CST

Five months.

I sit there thinking about that.

Why did he wait five months?

Maybe he was hoping she'd come back. Or maybe he was trying to figure out where to resend that first letter. But there's this awful nagging at the back of my head that keeps going, *Why did he wait?*

If it had been my kid, I would've been out there looking.

Subject: Alternate Universe of Bea (three)
From: Bea <b98989898@ymail.com>
To: Ezra <e89898989@ymail.com>
Date: Tues 23 Apr 10:16 CST

More from our father:

Anne. Please contact me. What you're doing constitutes kidnapping, only I don't hear you asking for ransom money. I don't hear you at all. She's my kid too. However I screwed things up, whatever I said, don't make Madelyn pay for it.

Madelyn.

Huh.

This letter, like all but one of the others, was never mailed. This one, like a lot of the others, mentions Madelyn.

As in *Bring Madelyn back.*

Let me see Madelyn.

Madelyn is my daughter too.

Madelyn is only three.

I didn't mean what I said about Madelyn being in the way.

You and Madelyn could never be a burden. I should never have said you were tying me down.

I may not have been a great husband, but I can be a great dad to Madelyn.

Madelyn.

Madelyn.

Madelyn.

Holy fuck.

Subject: Alternate Universe of Madelyn
From: Bea <b98989898@ymail.com>
To: Ezra <e89898989@ymail.com>
Date: Tues 23 Apr 10:42 CST

Madelyn Sierra Wooster was born August 22 at 6:33 pm in St. Luke's Hospital, St. Louis, Missouri. She weighed seven pounds, three ounces.

She was named for a great-aunt somewhere on her father's side and the California Sierras, honeymoon destination of Jonathan Calvin Wooster and Anne Vanessa Mathis.

Madelyn's first steps were at ten months old.

Her first word was "Up," delivered at age one, followed by "Yes" and, at fourteen months, an entire sentence: "I will do it myself."

She had her father's ears and nose and dark-blond hair. She had her mother's eyes, cheekbones, and large hands.

Her mom called her Maddy but her dad called her Bee because of the way she buzzed around the house once she started walking, and then running, and then running and humming at the same time.

Subject: Alternate Universe of Madelyn (two)

From: Bea <b98989898@ymail.com>

To: Ezra <e89898989@ymail.com>

Date: Tues 23 Apr 11:03 CST

HAVE YOU SEEN ME?

Madelyn Sierra Wooster

Date Missing: September 15

Missing From: St. Louis, MO

Age at Disappearance: 3

Sex: Female

Race: Caucasian

Height: 38"

Weight: 35 lbs.

Eyes: Brown

Hair: Blond/Brown

Other: Her ears are pierced. Sometimes answers to "Bee."

Circumstances:
Madelyn went missing from St. Louis, Missouri, on September 15, in the company of her mother (description available). She has not been seen or heard from since her disappearance.

Subject: Alternate Universe of Madelyn (three)
From: Bea <b989898898@ymail.com>
To: Ezra <e89898989@ymail.com>
Date: Tues 23 Apr 11:10 CST

I don't read them all. Not yet. They're just the same thing over and over. And I have this sinking feeling that makes me box them back up and slide them under Patch's bed. Don't get me wrong. It's so thoughtful of Dad to create a missing poster for his child. But did he actually do anything with it? Did he post it on street signs or store windows or on the internet?

I don't know.

But I can't shake the feeling that he could have done more. Like why didn't he at least file a police report? Why didn't he write more than sixteen letters? As far as I can tell, he loved me and wanted me back—shitty as it was to tell Mom I would be in the way—but was it that he really wanted me back? Okay, was it that he wanted *Madelyn* back? Or did he just want to punish Mom for taking me away?

My head is going round and round. I want to get drunk as hell and drown every thought, but then I would sober up and the thoughts would still be there, and I can't stay drunk the rest of my life, can I?

Can I?

I've chewed the skin around what remains of my nails so that it's cracked and bloody. Maybe I'll chew all the way up to my elbows or shoulders or head and make myself disappear. I wish I could make myself disappear.

But I did, didn't I? That's exactly what I did. Bea Ahern—gone. Madelyn Wooster—also gone. So that there's nothing left of either of me.

Subject: Alternate Universe of Madelyn (four)
From: Bea <b989898898@ymail.com>
To: Ezra <e89898989@ymail.com>
Date: Tues 23 Apr 11:18 CST

I'm sorry to write all this, Ez. At least he knew about me. I get that. I'm not trying to make you feel shittier than you already feel. I'm just falling apart and the world is upside down, and I need someone who's on my side. Not Patch, nice as he is. But someone who knows me. Not just someone—you.

Speaking of Patch. He'll be back any minute.

I slept with him. I wasn't going to tell you, but I'm trying to be honest in this new life of mine, and I don't have anyone else to tell. It isn't exactly the kind of thing I want to share with Franco.

I'll spare you the details, but it happened in his room last night after I emailed you. It wasn't my first time—that honor went to Joe—but it was my first time with someone more man than boy, who knows who he is and whose happiness doesn't seem to depend on me (I know how shitty and small that sounds, but we both know Joe has dependency issues).

Don't worry about Patch. He's one of the good ones. If anything, his friends should be warning him about me.

Love,
Your sister

p.s. I don't know why I said that. Habit maybe. I really like this guy. He's literally my best friend right now. You'd like him too. Maybe someday you'll get to meet him.

p.p.s. What if I fall in love with him?

p.p.p.s. I can't stay in his room much longer. Especially now that we're sleeping together. I'm just not sure where to go.

Subject: Unexpected allies

From: Ezra <e89898989@ymail.com>

To: Bea <b98989898@ymail.com>

Date: Tues 23 Apr 13:10 EST

I'm really happy you found Patch. Truly. I hope I get to meet him soon too.

I honestly don't know if I want to hear any more of our father's letters, though. Not only because I'm a non-person to him. (Although that doesn't feel great, as you can imagine.) I guess what I'm feeling is that the past can't help us now, Bea. Nothing in the past can help us. Whether he hung MISSING posters from sea to shining sea, or whether he just mocked one up to make himself feel better. Whether Mom had a solid reason to get away from him or whether Mom made the wrong decision and then kept running with it. Whether your name's been Madelyn or Martha or Beatrix or Anastasia, you are still the you you've become and I'm still the me I've become and there's no time machine that will ever make it otherwise. I know there are loose ends (like: we have a brother?), but I can't tie myself to them now. And I don't think you should, either. I know this sounds harsh, but I don't think it matters whether our father loved you or not. If there was no way for you to know that love, if there was no way for you to feel that love, if there was no way for that love to protect you or sustain you or give you a reason to fight another day . . . well, what good is it? I know shit about getting drunk, but I'm going to go out on a limb here and say: This isn't worth you getting drunk over. Especially not for the rest of your life. He doesn't deserve that. I'll say it again: The past can't help us now. What-ifs aren't going to help us forward; they're only going to drag us back.

Don't leave me for the Alternate Universe, Bea. I need your mind in this one.

Meanwhile, I'm here in school with plenty of people you already know.

Terrence has been wonderful (of course) and while I'm sure his parents are having plenty of whispered conversations about what to do about the fugitive they're harboring, Darren helped my argument immeasurably when he went after me on their front lawn. I don't think I'm going to be turned out anytime soon. But I know it's not a permanent solution. Terrence is talking like he thinks it is, but I know it isn't. I don't think he's prepared for all the sides of me he'll see if we're living together 24/7 for years. At a certain point, you can't feel like you have to be on your best behavior all the time when you're at home. And I will always feel like I should be on my best behavior in his house.

And speaking of people whose homes I've shared . . . Joe surprised me this morning at my locker. He came up to me all hangdog, and asked, "Are you avoiding me?"

I almost said, "Yes," and let that say everything, case closed.

But here's the thing, Bea. He genuinely looked sad about it. And I guess that reminded me he'd lost something too. It might have been an illusion, but losing illusions can hurt almost as much as losing people, I think.

When I didn't say anything right away, he added, "Look, I messed up. I get it. Your sister just gets to me, and I shouldn't have taken that out on you."

"It's fine," I said. And honestly, it was.

"You still have stuff at my house. Do you want me to bring it to you at Terrence's? That's where you are now, right?"

"Well, I certainly didn't go back to Mom and Darren."

"Thank God."

The way he said it, Bea—he'd seriously been worried that I'd gone back there. Or that I'd been sent back there.

"I'm never going back there," I told him. "To get the rest of my stuff, yes. To say my peace, maybe. But to live? Never. Never ever ever."

He clapped me on the shoulder. "Good." Then he looked me right in the eye and said, "You have no idea how much I wanted her to get out of there, Ezra. I would've done anything to get her out of there. That's the part of her leaving that I understand. I just don't know if I'll ever understand why she didn't ask me to help."

His body language was all *real talk*, so I decided I'd give him some real talk back. "Because you wouldn't have let her go, Joe," I said.

"I would've tried to get her to stay. Totally. But if she'd said no, if she'd said she had to get out of here, I would've helped her go."

"Okay," I said. What else could I say?

"So what I want to tell you is . . . I want to help you too. If you need me, I'm here. I'll be your driver, your backup, your friend. I owe you that."

"You don't owe me anything."

"No—that came out wrong. What I mean is, when I was recovering from the accident, a lot of it was on me, but there was another part that had to be a team effort. So when you get to that part that needs to be a team effort, I want to be on the team. That's what I'm saying."

"All right," I said. And as soon as he was gone, as soon as I had a moment to think, I started to understand how I was going to take him up on it.

A couple hours later, on my way to lunch, Jessica Wei stopped me.

"How are you doing?" she asked.

"I'm doing," I said.

She looked at me closely, tried to translate my tone.

"We still need to get coffee," she pointed out.

It wasn't a question, and I didn't need it to be.

I said sure.

I know you're probably thinking I should have plunged in right there, told her I needed us to skip lunch and go somewhere to talk. I have a feeling Jessica would have been down with that. But I'm not ready. That's the simple truth: I'm not ready. I know what's going to happen: She'll tell me her story, and I'll tell her my story. And maybe those two stories coming together will make us understand each of them better. Or maybe it won't, but at least we'll have someone to tell them to. I get that. But right now, there are parts of my story I feel I have to figure out before I show them to anyone else.

That's what I'm thinking about right now.

In my mind, tomorrow seems months away.

There's a lot I have to do first.

Subject: RE: Unexpected allies

From: Bea <b98989898@ymail.com>

To: Ezra <e89898989@ymail.com>

Date: Tues 23 Apr 15:27 CST

Dear Ez,

I just have to tell you about the last letter. It's from seven years ago. In it, Dad signs away his rights to us. He promises not to go after Mom or fight for custody or involve the police in getting us back. He just says okay, Anne, you can have them. I'm not going to fight you anymore.

That's what he says, Ez.

You can have them.

He gave up all rights to being our dad.

And then he doesn't even mail the letter.

He knew you existed. He knew where we were. He knew our names.

He couldn't even bother to officially give us up.

I was in the campus library when I read it. Patch was at practice and his roommate was in the room, and I had to find somewhere I could go, and it was easy enough to get another student to swipe me in with their ID. The people at the desk looked up and smiled at me and I smiled back, like oh, hey, like *yeah, I go here too,* and then I found a table up in the stacks and set the shoe box in front of me and started reading from where I left off.

It was more of the same—*Anne, talk to me. These are my kids too.* But the letters were fewer and farther between. And then finally this last one. He seemed to be answering her. Like they'd talked or she'd written, or her lawyer had written, and he just couldn't do it anymore. Fight for us. He was just done.

You can have them.

I laid my head down on the table and just cried. I cried for Madelyn and for Dad and for you and for me and even a little bit for Mom. I cried for Patch, who doesn't want to play basketball, and I cried for Joe, who nearly died, and for Sloane, who wouldn't have made out with Reggie Tan if I'd stayed at that party, and for Jessica Wei and for every person in the world who's struggling and suffering in silence, and I cried for London, who misses his dad—because let's face it, Jonathan Wooster was his dad, not ours—and then I cried for us again.

The thing I realized when I finally sat up—all these years I've been carrying around this little nugget of hope, buried somewhere deep inside, that maybe we weren't living the life we were supposed to, that maybe another, better life was waiting for us out there. I mean, who doesn't wish that at least once in their life? During all the shitty, shitty times with Darren and Mom, that little nugget of hope was the place I could go and curl up and tell myself, *It's okay. This isn't where you belong. There's something better for you out there. You don't belong here.*

And then you find out you did belong there all along, and there's nowhere you can go now because this is your life. Your shitty, fucked-up, dead-end life.

You can have them.

You can have them.

You can have them.

Subject: Have you seen me?
From: Bea <b98989898@ymail.com>
To: Ezra <e89898989@ymail.com>
Date: Wed 24 Apr 10:52 CST

Here is what I come away with: Dad was a decent-ish guy. He may not have tried hard enough, but for a while at least he tried to do the right thing. He probably would have been a lot easier to grow up with than Mom and Darren. But we'll never actually know.

Maybe at some point he just had to say, *I've got this other family, a wife and kid, so I'll just concentrate on them.* I think at some point he had to give up.

I tell Patch I need some air, and he drops me at Walmart, because of course I don't have a car and I don't have money for Uber or Lyft or even the bus. Not if I'm going to buy tampons and toothpaste.

So I'm in Walmart, and I walk and walk. I go down every aisle—even the gun aisle, even the tire aisle—and I try to breathe. At some point I realize my breath is amplified, like I'm on microphone, in and out, in and out. It's so *loud.* And people are looking, but all I can do is concentrate on not passing out. It's like suddenly everything I'm carrying around in my head and in my chest is expanding like an accordion, and there's no room for all of it inside me.

And then all at once the lights are too bright and the people are too loud, and there is too much stuff everywhere. I squint my eyes against it and hold my ears, trying to muffle the sound, and I head for the exit.

I'm starting to walk out, automatic doors opening, people behind me, and I freeze. Because taped to the window, the one by the doors, is this poster. It isn't very big—the size of a For Sale sign—but there are all these faces. Young faces. Kid faces. Some as young as four or five. Others as old as I am. *Have You Seen Me?* That's what it says at the top. And then below each picture, the name of the kid and the date they went missing, and where they were last seen and what they were wearing.

I study each face.

Kayla was allegedly abducted by her mother on July 5, 2017.

Elijah went missing from Woodland, California, on November 4, 2018, under suspicious circumstances.

Of course I'm not one of them. There's no picture of Beatrix Ahern, age eighteen, last seen wearing a red hoodie and faded jeans, missing since March of this year, or Madelyn Wooster, age three, missing for fifteen years.

King went missing from Gary, Indiana, on July 25, 2017.

Relisha went missing from Washington, DC, on March 19, 2016.

I'm frozen, practically committing these names and faces to

memory, and then I remember the people behind me, trying to get past, and I'm bumped and jostled as I move aside, and someone may swear at me under their breath. But it's okay because at least they see me.

"Have you seen me?" I ask the woman trying to juggle kids and bags as she gets around me.

She just stares at me and keeps juggling.

No, I think. How can you when I'm not even here? I'm Bea, I'm Madelyn, I'm missing, I'm a runaway, I was kidnapped by my own mother. I'm a high school dropout. A nobody. No one misses me except for you, Ezra. No one is looking for me because Dad is dead, and also, oh yeah, he just gave up. *You can have them.*

All of this—the faces on the door, every thought I'm having—gets me thinking about what it means to be seen. I feel like Terrence sees you pretty clearly, in a way Joe was never able to see me. I feel like the only person who's ever seen me clearly is you. Maybe that should be enough—to have one person who sees you. Some people probably don't even get that. And they probably don't see themselves. Am I Madelyn Wooster? Or Bea Ahern? Or both? I don't think I know who Beatrix Ellen Ahern Madelyn Sierra Wooster is. Maybe I never will.

I leave Walmart and start walking. I walk right past Patch, waiting in his car, and head down the street toward I don't know where. I hear the horn behind me and ignore it. I tell myself, *Why should I wait for him? He'll only leave too. They always leave, don't they?* I guess technically I left you and then I left Franco, and in a way I left London. So maybe if Patch doesn't leave me, I'll leave him because it's in my blood and that's just what I do.

I walk and then I start to run, and I'm going nowhere, Ez, but I'm telling myself I'm running *to* something. Maybe I'm running to Beatrix Ellen Ahern Madelyn Sierra Wooster. Or maybe I'm just running to nowhere, after all this time. Maybe that's where I belong.

I slept in the daybed at Franco's, cocooned by the pillows, trying my best to disappear. I still had the key he gave me, and I didn't think twice about using it. I felt like he wouldn't mind somehow, like he'd rather I stay there than on the street.

I woke up with him standing over me, ear hair twitching, dark eyes flashing.

He let out a stream of Italian, so loud I had to cover my ears.

I got up, made the bed while he yelled at me. I put the pillows back in place. I pulled on my shoes. So calm. I was so calm. I know what to do when people yell at you. Hugs, no. Niceness, no. Yelling, yeah, I get that.

At some point he switched to English, and he calmed down a little, but by then I was halfway across the store heading to the door.

"Beatrix," he said. It was enough to stop me from leaving.

"What?"

"Stop running."

I didn't say anything because I wasn't going to cry, even though I wanted to because he would have hated it.

"Stop running. No more running." His voice was quiet then. Like he was suddenly leading a meditation or teaching yoga. "No more running. We were worried, Irene and me. We don't know where you go or if you're okay."

"I'm sorry." And I actually stood there resenting him, resenting the two of them for caring about me.

"No more running. If you don't want to stay here anymore, we need to know that you're somewhere safe. You are young. But you've already lived a life. More than you should. But you have so much life to come. If you are safe." He rubbed at his eyebrows, what was left of the hair on his head. "It's been a long time since we worried about one of our children. They're grown, they're gone. They are okay. But now we worry about you."

Now we worry about you.

There was a boulder-size lump in my throat. It was all I could do to say, "I'm sorry."

"No more running. You won't get anywhere with all that running."

For just a second—light as a feather—he rested a hand on my shoulder. And then he took that hand and patted me so hard on the back that I almost fell over.

I called Patch from the store and he came to get me. Without me telling him where I wanted to go, he headed for campus. He turned the music (Tupac) up loud and we rode the whole way without talking.

It wasn't until he parked the truck and shut off the engine that I said, "I'm not going in there with you until you talk to me." I meant *in there* as in his dorm.

"Okay," he said. "Let's talk about you just taking off yesterday."

"Sorry." But it didn't sound like I was because I wasn't really.

"That's it?"

"That's it." And I don't know, Ez, I was just so tired by this point. Which is why I said, "It's not like I owe you anything." And my heart started racing because I kind of do owe him. I mean, he helped me out when no one else would, not counting Franco and Irene.

"Nice."

"What?"

He sits back against his door, staring at me and shaking his head. "You act like you're this hard-ass who never feels anything."

"Maybe I am. Maybe I don't."

He's still shaking his head. "Yeah, but we both know that's not true. At some point, you gotta just own it, Martha. You've got a heart. And it's been hurt. And you'd rather hurt someone else than have them hurt you, but then you're only hurting yourself."

"Did you learn that in Psychology 101?"

"No. It's pretty fucking obvious. And I'm not stupid." This is the first time I've heard him swear, and it kind of gets to me. Like this is what a bad influence I am and I've pushed him past his limits.

He slams out of the car, and I sit there for a minute trying to decide what to do, and then there's this rapping on the window and I nearly jump out of my skin. Patch is waving at me like *come on*. So I get out and wait for him to storm off toward the dorm, not speaking, but instead he takes my hand, twining his fingers through mine, and this is how we walk across campus. I keep looking down at my hand in his, expecting it to evaporate, leaving my hand clutching nothing but air. But it doesn't.

"What about Everly?" I say. Because some part of me needs him to tell me *again* that there is no Everly. That there's only Martha and Patch.

"Fuck Everly," he says. Together we walk to the dorm.

And the thing is, Ez, he's right—not about Everly but about me ultimately hurting myself. And I know he's right. And he knows I know he's right.

Which is why there's a lot I have to do too.

Subject: Your heart

From: Ezra <e89898989@ymail.com>

To: Bea <b98989898@ymail.com>

Date: Wed 24 Apr 12:15 EST

The boy's right. You do have a heart. And it has been hurt.

Part of the hurt's come from that nugget of hope—so many nuggets of hope—bouncing around in there.

Yes, Dad gave up on you. Mom did at some point, too.

But fuck it, Bea. I didn't.

And you know what?

NEITHER.

DID.

YOU.

So Dad said, *You can have them.*

So Mom acted like having us wasn't exactly a prize.

So Darren clearly wished he didn't have to be with us at all.

So. What.

Your heart is stronger than any of the hurts inflicted. Even the ones that were self-inflicted.

Don't believe me? Put your hand right there on your chest.

Pledge of allegiance, to yourself. What's that heart doing? What's it saying to you?

I thought so.

Now, my heart needs some answers.

More soon.

Subject: This is how it ends and begins

From: Ezra <e89898989@ymail.com>

To: Bea <b98989898@ymail.com>

Date: Wed 24 Apr 22:22 EST

So there's a lot to tell you here. I'm trying to remember it all.

Here goes:

School ends. I tell Terrence I've made plans with Joe. He looks a little surprised, but also doesn't want to act like me living with him means I have to spend every moment with him. I'm counting on that.

I texted Joe right after I emailed you earlier.

I needed a driver.

First I have Joe drive me to the house, to make sure she isn't there.

Then I have him drive me to her office.

I'm betting that now that tax season is over, it's going to be understaffed. I remember how she used to talk about that all the time over dinner, how the accountants' summer started on April 16th. Not that she ever treated it like summer with us.

I deliberately wait until it's after five. Her car is in the parking lot with only two others. When I walk inside, the receptionist desk is empty. That room, the reception room, is the one I remember the most. Because whenever there was a school closing or something and she had to take us to work, that's where she'd park us for the whole day. Remember how boring that was? I swear, it looks like they still have the same magazines. I almost open one up to see if I can find any scribbles of ours. Then I realize the only reason I remembered there'd be scribbles was because of the way we were yelled at for scribbling in them. Not in the reception area, not with anyone else around. But the minute we got in the car. I remember being so ashamed. I remember feeling like I'd ruined everything, that all the people who'd been nice to us in the reception area over the last few hours probably thought we were monsters now. We'd ruined their magazines!

I have to wander around a little to find her actual office. I don't have any real memories of doing anything fun there, just waiting obediently for her to finish up so we could go. I double-check to make sure my phone is on, just in case I have to prepare Joe for a speedy getaway.

The door has that frosted glass, so I can see her moving around inside. It sounds like she's getting ready to leave. I stand there for a second, watching this blurry version of her, our mother reduced to color and movement, just the suggestion of a person. Then I open the door and see her for real.

The opening of the door startles her, and my presence startles her even more.

Does she say my name?

Does she say how sorry she is?

Does she thank God that I'm back?

No. She says, "What are you doing here?" Like I'm something that's fallen off the shelf of her past, breaking on the floor of her present.

"I'm here to talk," I say. "That's all."

Neutral ground, Bea. I figured this would be neutral ground. I want this to be a business transaction, not a scene. And maybe I thought she'd still have a little of her professional demeanor from the day, like when someone from work would call the house and when she was talking to them, she sounded like the most level-headed, reasonable person you could ever expect to find.

I was right about her getting ready to leave. Her jacket is in her hand, her purse on her shoulder.

She says, "If you want to talk, you can come to the house later, when we're all present."

We're all. I notice that you aren't included in this tally. But I don't point that out because, as I said, I'm trying to keep it professional.

"No," I tell her. "I only want to talk to you."

I'm not intentionally blocking the doorway, but the reality is that I'm blocking the doorway.

I can see her make the calculation—other people might still be around, and it's probably better to have me in a contained environment. She gestures me in, then puts her jacket and her purse down on a side chair as I close the door behind me.

She goes to the other side of her desk, and for a second I think she's going to sit down and tell me to sit down across from her, like I'm here to talk about an audit, or to set financial planning goals for the next tax year. But she stays standing. She wants the desk between us.

"I don't know what to say to you," she states. "Ever since your sister left, you have acted deplorably. I hoped that her departure would have freed you of her influence, but instead it seems to have amplified it."

"This isn't about her."

"Isn't it? She's trying to turn you against us. And you'll believe everything she says. Beatrix can do no wrong in your eyes. But she can do *plenty* wrong, Ezra. You just refuse to see it."

"That's not true!" I argue.

She looks at me the same way she must've when I'd been learning to spell and had assumed *cat* started with a *k*. "Let me guess," she says. "You came here to accuse me and Darren of ruining your life. Or of being horrible parents. You'd much rather have been with your father. Your sainted, blameless father. Or maybe you would have been better off on your own. That's apparently how Bea feels. And whatever she feels, you'll feel too. You were always like that, following her around, mimicking her actions. She needed a Band-Aid, you wanted one. She insisted she had a fever, then you insisted you were hot. And when I took your temperature and showed you both you didn't have fevers, that didn't matter. All that mattered was what your sister *felt.* I had thought you'd outgrow it, and for a while it seemed like you had. She went out of control, but you didn't veer after her. That was a relief. But not now, Ezra—now you're both being awful."

This feels a little one-sided to me. "*We're* being awful?" I spit out. "Darren practically knocks me out in front of Terrence's neighbors the other day, and *we're* the ones being awful."

"You're awful when you provoke us. You can't say you haven't provoked us. Setting the house on fire! I had to pretend that I'd left the paper towels near an open flame. That's what I told the fire department. Covering for you, Ezra. You. And the childish things you did to the things in my purse—that's what a four-year-old does to get attention. I think it's more than understandable that Darren was upset at your behavior, and how ungrateful you've been behaving. All you had to do was get into the car when we asked, Ezra. After what you did with the fire, I think it was incredibly forgiving of us to invite you back. Darren was so mad at you, and I didn't blame him. But he was willing to let you come home. He told me that. You just threw it back in his face."

"I can't believe we're having this conversation! Can you hear yourself?"

"I know you think you know everything, Ezra, but you don't. I'm sorry, but you don't. Darren has been my rock in more ways than you can ever know. He saved our family after your father's cruelty. I could not have done it on my own. I only had so much to give, and you both had *so* much to take. Sometimes I told myself your father had no idea. But other times I thought he knew exactly what he was doing, leaving just when it was getting hard. Well, Darren was up to that challenge. If I'd been him, I would've run far, far away, but he didn't run. He loved me when I thought no one would. And he still does. It's not my fault if you kids never liked that. You wanted me all to yourself, and that's just not the way it works, Ezra. Darren's always tried very hard to treat you and Bea as if you were his own children, even though you have never made the least attempt to treat him that way in return."

I can't help it. I yell, "Are you fucking kidding me?"

Predictably, she bursts out with, "Watch your language!"

Remember the time Darren said that to you, and you said, "How can I watch something that's not visible? Are there subtitles I should be seeing?"

I almost say the same thing now. But instead I go with, "No, Mom, you watch *your* language. You watch every *fucking* lie that comes out of your mouth. When I was four or ten or even fourteen, I might have believed them. Not now."

She pounds her hand on her desk. "I don't have to stand here and be insulted—"

I pound her desk right back. "YES YOU DO. You have to stand there and tell me why you chose to love him and not us.

You have to stand there and listen to me when I say that it never made sense to us, how he could be so good to you and so awful to us. You have to stand there and explain why you hid us from our father. You have to make me understand why you have stood there and stood there and stood there while Darren attacked us and destroyed our things and undermined us and hurt us and made sure we'd never, ever feel welcome in our own home. You want to tell me that he's your rock? He saved you? Well, that *shouldn't have been enough.* I don't get it—you *stole us from our father.* And for what? So we could suffer on your terms instead of his? Bea found him, Mom. We know what happened."

She shakes her head. "You have no idea. No idea whatsoever."

"Of what? *Tell me.*"

It's like something in her cracks open in front of my eyes. After living with her and studying her my whole life, somehow she comes up with a new expression, a look of such clarity and ferocity. We know what a mama bear looks like defending her cub. But what does she look like defending herself against her cub? "You have no idea what your father was like!" she yells. "You have *no idea* what he did to us. I protected the two of you from that. If there's one thing you need to give me credit for, it is that. Even your cold, vicious, self-centered hearts have to recognize that. I have no idea how Bea found your father or what he's been saying to her, but let me tell you, he never put your interests above his own. He was the one who wanted kids in the first place, but then when he had them, he changed his mind. He said

I'd *tied him down*—well, let me tell you, Ezra, if I tied him down, I didn't do a very good job on the knots. When I was pregnant with your sister, there'd be nights he wouldn't come home, and his excuses wouldn't even bother to dress themselves as excuses. No, they'd come clothed as blame. Maybe he said he was looking elsewhere because I was being a drag. Maybe he said he had to have a night out because he couldn't stand another night in. The man who didn't spend a single minute trying to understand me was always ready to point out that I didn't understand him. And do you know what kind of fool I was? I tried to make it better! Whatever he may tell you now, I worked my ass off and burned out all my instincts in order to please him, in order to get him to stay. I made the meals. I never complained. I told him he was right even when he was wrong. And do you know how well that worked? When I told him I was pregnant with you, he responded by saying he'd already made another woman pregnant, and that he couldn't be in both places at once. So guess which place won, Ezra. Guess why you never saw your father. If now, fifteen years later, you and your sister want to measure us against one another, I'm sure I'll lose, because I did a thousand things wrong while he did nothing at all. He didn't deserve to be a part of your lives. If I was going to shoulder the burden, he was not going to have any part of the reward. Nothing you can say will convince me otherwise. He knew what he was doing the whole time. And now if he's waltzing in, saying he's the better parent—well, I'm sorry. I'm not going to accept that. And if you're going to accept that, then I'm sorry I've raised such an ungrateful child."

I react to the only part I know how to react to in that moment. I tell her, "He's not waltzing in."

She practically rolls her eyes. "No? Then what is he doing, reaching out now?"

"He didn't reach out. He's dead."

At that moment, another new expression rises to the surface. But it doesn't clarify into something solid. It wavers. She holds her hand out to her desk chair for balance. "What?"

My tone goes from attack to explanation. "He's dead. He died last year."

"But your sister—"

"Bea went out there because our brother contacted her. The one who's my age."

"I have to sit down," she says, then does just that. "I don't understand."

"My father's dead. But honestly, this doesn't have anything to do with him. This is about things that were there long before we found out about him."

"How can this not have anything to do with him? What are you saying, Ezra?"

"I'm saying this is about Darren."

She lets go of the arm of the chair and puts her hand up to stop me. "No. Stop. I will not have you spew your ingratitude now. This isn't the time for it."

Now it's my turn to be exasperated. "It's never the time for it."

"Darren has always treated me well."

"I know. But he hasn't always treated *us* well."

"Because you haven't treated *him* well."

"But we're the *children*!"

Mom shakes her head. "Bea hasn't been a child for years. She's been a selfish, combative teenager who's wrung every ounce of happiness from our family."

"Do you believe that? Do you honestly believe that?"

She sighs. "Yes, Ezra. I do."

"All those times Darren has yelled at us, has been cruel to us—even when he was pummeling me on Sunday—you think it's *our* fault?"

"I'm not saying I always approve of the way he handles things. I've talked to him about that. But you provoke him. The two of you always provoke him."

"How do we provoke him?"

"Trying to burn down our house? Stealing from me? Having him *arrested,* Ezra? If those aren't provocations, I don't know what they are."

"How about self-defense?"

She actually laughs at that. *"Please."*

That's what does it, Bea. I realize she will never, ever see things our way. Even if she's right about our father—and I have a sinking suspicion she is—it doesn't excuse everything that came after. It might explain it, but it doesn't excuse it.

"You have to let Darren go," I say, knowing exactly the response I will get.

Sure enough, she replies, "I'm not going to do that. Why would I do that?"

"Then you're going to have to let me go. Bea's already gone. Now I'm going to go too."

"Don't be ridiculous. You may be choosing at this moment to block out all of the good times we've had together. You may be choosing to ignore the fact that we've raised you, supported you, and given you a lot of the qualities you now think are so diametrically opposed to us. You can conveniently erase all of that, just like your sister chose to do. But you can't change the simple fact that we're your family."

Where has she been living all these years, Bea? What has she been seeing?

I say, "You never listen to me, but you need to listen to me now. Because this is what I'm saying: You're not my family anymore. I have Bea. I have Terrence and his family. I have other friends, and I will find other family. If you want this to be ugly, we can make this really ugly. You can try to force me to come home. And I can call the police every time Darren threatens me or goes on the attack. I can make sure everyone in town knows what's happening, and no matter what trash you try to spread about me, the truth will stick at least some of the time to you. Right now, I hate you both. I don't want to. I don't want to live like that. I will never feel anything other than hate for him. But for you? I might get to pity, and go from there. Time will tell. But for now, I'm out. As soon as I walk through that door, you are going to call Darren and have him take you to dinner. While you're at the restaurant of your choosing, I will take two hours to go to our house and take the things I want from my room. Eventually Bea may come back for hers—I don't know. What I do know is that your position of mom is no longer an automatic right. It is something that you need to earn. Starting now."

Her voice is calm. Certain. "I'm your mother. I'll always be your mother."

"Yes," I concede, "you control that fact. But I get to control what it means."

She pushes back in her chair and stares at me. "How did I raise two such unforgiving children?"

And this time I'm the one who laughs. Especially since she genuinely doesn't seem to know.

"I think it's something we learned at home," I say.

At that moment, she does the thing that almost destroys me. She looks at a frame on her desk, and from where I'm standing, I can see it's a picture of us, Bea. Us next to each other on a swing set, you higher in the air, me giggling near the ground. Nobody is pushing us. We're swinging on our own.

"I'm going now," I say gently. "If you want to call me in order to yell or demand or threaten, please don't bother. If you want to call me to talk, I might not answer at first. But eventually I might. We'll see."

She doesn't nod. She doesn't shake her head. She doesn't react at all. It's like she's listening to music in another room.

Only when I get to the door does she say something.

"Is he really dead?" she asks.

"Yes."

"Are you sure your sister isn't making that up?"

"I'm sure," I say. "Bea would never lie to me about that."

She shakes her head again. I think she believes me, but can't believe the world.

I leave the room. I like to think she notices I'm gone.

Sorry, just need to take a moment here.

Okay. What comes next. I hold my feelings in as I walk through the office, just in case I bump into someone. Joe is still waiting in the parking lot. He starts to barrage me with questions as soon as I get into the car.

"Drive," I say. *"Go."*

To his credit, he doesn't say anything for a minute or two. Then he breaks the silence to ask, "Where are we going?"

I don't start crying until I say, "Home."

• • •

I tell him to stand guard, but he insists on coming in with me. Because we have no idea what Mom will do. If she tells Darren, he'll storm in as soon as he can.

"I've got your back," Joe says, like we're in a war movie. It's both nice and annoying at the same time.

At some point since I've last been in the house, my room has been pillaged in the same way yours had been pillaged. "Jesus," Joe mutters as we walk in to see the contents of my drawers piled in the middle of the floor.

"I need some trash bags," I say.

"I'll get them," Joe offers. And I think, oh yeah, he probably knows where they are.

I only have about two minutes alone in that room, two minutes to size up fifteen years and decide what's worth keeping. Was that how you felt, Bea, the night you left? How did you know what to take and what to abandon?

Joe comes back with a whole box of leaf bags.

"Err on the side of keeping," he says. (I mean, of course he does.)

But you know what? I listen to him. I take everything that's meant even a little bit to me. I leave behind shirts I never wear and books I'll never read again. When I find a cache of old birthday cards, from before Darren, I take one or two Mom gave me. I wonder if she'll notice.

I take anything that's from you.

When I'm done, and have made detours to the bathroom

and the den, we have six very full trash bags. Joe brings them down to the car while I make sure I haven't missed anything. My room already doesn't feel like mine anymore. It's just another room in Mom and Darren's house.

Before he lugs the last bag down, Joe says, "I guess they're not coming."

I nod. I don't think either of us truly believed we could do this without a fight.

While he takes that last bag of mine to the car, I go into your room with another bag. I try to pick some things I know you once loved—Stella the Unicorn and the Monopoly we always played with the handmade pieces and maybe a drawing or two I made you when I was little; I figure if they've lasted this long, they deserve to last a little longer. There are some photos of you and Joe, and you and Sloane, and you and some kids I don't recognize—I take those too. Better for you to have them than for Mom and Darren to get rid of them.

I also take all of your Anne of Green Gables books. If you don't want them, I'll take them. I borrowed them enough, way back when.

I hear a cough outside the door and nearly jump out of my skin. But it's only Joe, keeping his distance, as if your room is a sacred space. I know it isn't sacred to you anymore, but maybe it still is to him and to me. I'm sure he wants me to invite him in, but I don't. I just tell him I'm ready to go.

Most of the bags are now in Joe's garage. I didn't think it

would be a good look for me to show up at Terrence's house with seven large garbage bags of stuff. I'm starting with one, and we'll go from there.

Terrence was a little miffed when I told him what I'd done with Joe. I made it sound like Joe got the job because he could drive. But honestly? There are still some things about our family that I hope Terrence never sees. I don't want that much of our history to be there whenever he looks at me. I want him to be part of what comes after, not what came before.

(Who knows? Maybe Patch will be like that for you.)

So, last thoughts: What's unnerving me now, what's making me upset, isn't what I've done—it's the uncertainty of what comes next. I'm exhausted, Bea. Completely exhausted. But of course I had to tell you all this before I went to bed.

Right now, you're the only family I have.

Subject: Family

From: Bea <b98989898@ymail.com>

To: Ezra <e89898989@ymail.com>

Date: Wed 24 Apr 23:22 CST

Dear Ezra,

This is your big sister. Everything is going to be okay. More soon. I love you.

Love,

Me

Subject: Apology from Bea

From: Bea <b98989898@ymail.com>

To: footballjoe08@gmail.com

Date: Thurs 25 Apr 00:01 CST

Dear Joe,

I don't know how to start this email, so here goes. Thank you for being on Ezra's team. It means a lot to him and a lot to me. You've been a really good friend to both of us, even though I haven't always been the friend you deserve.

Which brings me to:

I'm sorry for everything. I'm sorry I left without a word. I'm sorry I hurt you. I'm good now, but I had to get out for reasons you may or may not understand. Trouble at home. I'm sorry I didn't tell you about it when we were together.

I should have been honest with you about a lot of things. And I never should have stayed with you just because of your accident. You deserve more.

Love,

Bea

Subject: From Bea

From: Bea <b98989898@ymail.com>

To: terrrrrrence@gmail.com

Date: Thurs 25 Apr 00:14 CST

Hi Terrence,

Thank you for standing up for Ez. I know you didn't do it for me, but I want to tell you how much I appreciate it. All of it. I'm overdue in thanking you for all you and your parents are doing for him. I know you were never my biggest fan, but there was a lot we couldn't tell anyone. Not you, not Joe. I hope you understand that and never hold it against Ez. From what I know of you through him, you never would. You're lucky to have each other.

And you're lucky to have nice parents who use words for something other than threats or comments about what a letdown you are as a human. I'm guessing they don't believe in hitting either.

Gratefully yours,

Bea x

Subject: from your old best friend

From: Bea <b98989898@ymail.com>

To: sloanexxxx@gmail.com

Date: Thurs 25 Apr 00:36 CST

Sloane,

Yes, it's me. Bea. A voice from beyond the grave.

I want to say I'm sorry I left the way I did and I'm sorry for not telling you I was leaving. I'm sorry I didn't tell you a lot of other things too.

I hope you're okay. No hard feelings about Joe. No hard feelings at all. Life's too short.

xx

Bea

Subject: from your daughter
From: madelynwooster@ymail.com
To: anneahern72@gmail.com
Date: Thurs 25 Apr 01:03 CST

Dear Anne,

This is your daughter.

Beatrix Ellen Ahern, just to remind you in case you've forgotten.

I'm the one who lived with you for eighteen years and recently left you and Darren and the hell home you created together. The daughter you never thought would amount to much. The one you gave up on years ago.

I'm not sure why you gave up on me. Maybe it was me, although it's hard to imagine giving up on a five-year-old. That's how far back the memories go. You being disappointed. You being angry. You giving me the cold shoulder. You freezing me out for hours and then days. You telling me just how disappointing I was. Telling me everything you'd done for me, and this is how I thank you. When I was *five.* And too young to know how to make you happy.

Or.

Maybe it was you. Maybe you just weren't meant to be a mother. Didn't you tell me that more than once? *I never should've had kids.*

Not that I want to wish away my own existence, but I'm going to have to agree with you. You never should have had them.

It has come to my attention that once upon a time you wanted me enough to take me from my father, who apparently didn't want me, but then later changed his mind and *did,* or so he said. And then you had Ezra and our dad eventually found out, but by then you apparently wanted us so badly you changed my name and our last name and hid us away and refused to let him have any sort of relationship with his children. Or maybe it wasn't about us? Maybe it was about him? Maybe you were just punishing him for not wanting me in the first place.

Either way, and whatever reason you may have had, it completely and utterly sucks. You think you know who you are for all of your life and suddenly you learn you're someone else with a different name and a dad who was good, and that you could have had this completely different life. Which is something you've literally dreamed about forever—a different life. Any life other than the one you have.

We could have had that, Ezra and me. We deserved to know our dad. He died last year. He looked for us but now we'll never get to know him. If you didn't want us, why couldn't you have let us stay with him? We could have lived with him, a person who actually wanted us, and loved you from afar.

Anytime you want to start being a mom, be my guest. Not for me—that ship has sailed—but for Ezra, your son.

Sincerely,
Madelyn Sierra Wooster

p.s. This email address will self-destruct in twenty-four hours. I don't expect you to write back. I don't need you to write back. I wrote this to let you know how I feel.

Subject: from the all-knowing Martha

From: Bea <b989898898@ymail.com>

To: patchaaronr@gmail.com

Date: Thurs 25 Apr 11:14 CST

Dear Patch:

Thank you for being on my side when I needed it most. At the risk of sounding sappy, you'll never know how much that means to me.

Don't let that go to your head.

Anyway, I'll see you later tonight so I'll keep this brief. I just had to say that. And also this:

Life is short. It's too short to try to make other people happy by living their dreams. Trust me on this. As you know, in addition to being extraordinarily hot, I'm wise beyond my years, and I know this from experience. Not the dreams part, because I never really had any of those until now, but the trying-to-make-other-people-happy part. Here's the thing about trying to make them happy—the people who want you to make them happy usually aren't happy people to begin with. If they're asking you to do something you don't want to do, something that's not really in you, they're only going to be happy for like a minute before they find something else they need you to do for them.

As someone once told me, if you don't like your life, change it. Stop bitching and be the change you want to see in the world. You're made for bigger things.

Why not just say, *Hey, Dad, I love you, and I know you want me to play basketball, but it would make me miserable.* The way I look at it, it's him or you in this case, and sometimes you've got to choose you.

End of lecture.

Oh, and by the way, you snore. You say you don't, but you do. *Loudly.*

It's okay, though. It makes you a little less perfect and a little less handsome, and therefore easier to be around.

See you soon.

Love,
Bea (aka the person formerly known as Martha) xx

Subject: from your disappearing friend Bea Ahern

From: Bea <b98989898@ymail.com>

To: franco@francositmarket.com

Date: Thurs 25 Apr 13:28 CST

Dear Franco:

I'm sorry I left like I did. You and Irene are the nicest people I've ever known, and all you've done is show me kindness at the time I needed it most. But then I guess we all need kindness, no matter what we're going through. So it's not that your kindness was only because you felt sorry for this poor, lost girl, it was because that's who you are.

I'm writing to let you know I'm okay. And to ask if I could come back to work for you. I would also love to rent my old room again, if it's available, but I understand if you don't feel like taking another chance on an employee and tenant who didn't say goodbye. No hard feelings if you can't do it. I will always be grateful to you for everything you've done for me.

But I am going to stay in St. Louis. And I would like to save money for college. This may be a long shot, but I'm not going to think about the things I might not be able to do. That's something I've been told all my life—what I can't do. I'm ready to see what I can do.

Your friend,
Bea

Subject: graduation and school-related questions from Beatrix Ahern
From: Bea <b98989898@ymail.com>
To: VPSoutherly@whcommunityschools.edu
Date: Thurs 25 Apr 13:54 CST

Dear Vice Principal Southerly:

To answer your question, yes, there has been trouble at home. There has been trouble at home for many, many years. This doesn't excuse the fact that I left school several weeks ago, but that trouble at home is one of the primary reasons for my absence.

I know we are three weeks away from graduation, and I've missed more time than that, but I wanted to find out if there is a chance of making up that work. If there is, do I reach out to my teachers directly or is that something you would do? If it's too late for me to graduate with my class, is there a summer school option? Or would you recommend that I take the GED? I've already taken the SAT.

Any information you can send me would be amazing. I'm actually thinking about applying to college, and I want to figure out what I need and if this is really, truly a possibility for me.

All my life I've been told I'd never amount to anything. Almost everyone I know has written me off. That's not an excuse, but it's the truth. And I think I wrote myself off too. But I'm not doing that anymore.

One last thing. If you had your suspicions that trouble existed at home—which apparently you did—Ezra and I would have appreciated your support. We can't be the only students you've ever met with rotten parents and rotten home lives, but hopefully next time you'll trust your instincts and press harder, dig deeper, and refuse to give up until you find out what's really going on.

Sincerely,
Beatrix Ahern

Subject: update from your sister

From: Bea <b98989898@ymail.com>

To: LONDON WOOSTER <l89989889@ymail.com>

Date: Thurs 25 Apr 14:12 CST

Dear London,

Thanks for showing me your house the other day and for introducing me to your mom. Please tell her thank you too.

So it looks like I'm staying in St. Louis for a while. It's going to take me some time to adjust to being here, as in *being here,* an actual Missouri resident, and I'm not sure how often we can see each other. I don't want to cut you out of my life, but this whole thing has turned my life upside down and I just don't know how much I can do right now or how much I'll be able to do down the road. I'm not sure what exactly you want from me, but I have to decide what I can do and what I can't do. I want to be honest with you because if we're going to have any sort of relationship, that's important.

I promise not to disappear completely, though.

And who knows? Maybe we'll meet again at the turtle park.

Sending you a hug and one for your mom. You're a good kid and whatever happens, I'm glad I met you.

Love,

Bea

Subject: from Madelyn
From: Bea <b98989898@ymail.com>
To: Bea <b98989898@ymail.com>
Date: Thurs 25 Apr 14:51 CST

Dear Dad:

I would never have given up on you. I know that's easy for me to say, but it's true. I'm sorry you gave away your rights to us but thank you for trying to find Ezra and me, at least for a while. I hope your life was happy. I hope you loved Amelia and that she loved you, and that you really were as good a dad as London says.

I wish I'd gotten to know you, but I guess I got to know you a little and that's something.

Don't worry about Ezra and me. We're good. In spite of everything we've been through and everything we're dealing with, in spite of Darren and Mom and our whole shitty childhood, we're going to be fine. We really are. I believe that now.

We're going to be fucking great.

Love,
Bee

Subject: Dear Madelyn

From: Bea <b98989898@ymail.com>

To: Bea <b98989898@ymail.com>

Date: Thurs 25 Apr 15:22 CST

Dear Madelyn:

I see you.

I am you.

But not you.

Because I'm me. The me who doesn't remember the father you had. The me who lived with Mom all these years and never knew anyone ever cared about finding me or that I was even lost at all.

Maybe I'm still lost.

Or maybe I'm not.

Maybe I'm right where I should be. And maybe I wouldn't have gotten here if all these things hadn't happened, if I hadn't been lost and then found, lost and then found.

Okay, I'm not usually this poetic. But you get the picture.

I'm sorry your mom stole you, but if I hadn't lived the life I did—my life, not yours—I wouldn't be this me.

And actually? This me isn't bad. In fact, I like her.

For the first time ever, I really like her.

Love,

Bea

Subject: Family
From: Bea <b98989898@ymail.com>
To: Ezra <e89898989@ymail.com>
Date: Thurs 25 Apr 18:01 CST

Dear Ez:

As I said, it's all going to be okay. You're going to be okay, and I'm going to be okay, and we're going to be okay. I know you're exhausted and I know you're uncertain. I am too. But I'm also really fucking proud of us for getting out of there and away from Mom and Darren. That's not easy to do, and it's not something we can do alone, much as we hate needing other people.

I'm going to stay here in St. Louis. I'm terrified and excited and I have no fucking clue what's going to happen. But at least I'm deciding for myself.

If you need me, I can come back. Literally, I will get on a bus and be there. Just say the word. Or you can come here. I'll always have a place for you. This is not me saying goodbye. It's me deciding for myself.

I've written to Mom. It ended up being a little less angry than expected, but I laid it out there. I haven't heard from her, but I didn't expect to. Sometimes you just need to say it.

I'm also talking to Southerly about making up my classes so that maybe, just maybe, I can graduate. I'm moving back into Franco's, and my address will be:

Beatrix Ahern
c/o Franco's Italian Market
5183 Wilson Avenue
St. Louis, MO 63110

I was also able to buy a burner phone. Maybe we could talk? The number is 314-555-2322. Oh, and I have a new email: beatrixahern@gmail.com. You can use that one from now on or you can use this one. I won't get rid of it because I'm kind of attached to it now. It's been my lifeline to you.

I love you, Ez. You are my family and the most important person to me in this world.

Oh, and one more thing.

It's wonderful when someone else sees you, the real you, but—and this may be the most profound thing I've ever thought or said—maybe the important thing is seeing yourself.

My vision has always been clouded by how others saw me—Mom, Darren, Joe, Sloane, my teachers. It's easy to start seeing yourself as others do, to believe the reflection they paint for you, but for the first time ever I'm looking at myself. *Who is Bea?* She's funny and smart. Smarter than she ever thought. She's resourceful and resilient and she can figure things out on her own.

She can be a hard worker. She can be sexy. (Sorry you had to hear that, Ez, but it's true.) She actually has a good laugh. She likes to laugh. She wants to learn. She wants to be a good sister. She wants to be a kind person who helps others. She doesn't want to be an island all to herself. She wants to be able to cry and have someone tell her it's going to be okay, even if she doesn't need them to.

For the first time, I like what I see.

Love,
Your sister
Bea x

Subject: Over coffee

From: Ezra <e89898989@ymail.com>

To: Bea <b989889898@ymail.com>

Date: Thurs 25 Apr 19:34 EST

How weird that you had to travel all that way to see the Bea I know. But I get it. Sometimes that's what it takes. I'm glad you found her.

I won't lie: I wish you were here. I understand why you're not, and I'm going to live with why you're not. But the wish will always be there.

Meanwhile, there's this:

I finally had coffee with Jessica Wei. We met up after school, and as soon as we were out of range of everyone else, the conversation started.

"You're not still living at home, are you?" she asked.

I said no, I was living at Terrence's for now.

"Good," she said. "That's a relief."

Then she started to talk about how she and Terrence had been friends when they were little kids, and how she'd loved it over there because for some reason her mom didn't think Play-Doh was a good idea, while Terrence's mom bought fresh Play-Doh every week, it seemed. I thought, okay, now we're talking about being kids, so I tried to find some good stories to tell back to her, although it was a stretch. Mostly I focused on crafts projects we had in school, the ones I'd never bring home because I knew there was no way Mom or Darren would hang them up on the refrigerator. There was this one box I made out of Popsicle sticks—I hid it under my bed and it got all dusty. Mom must've thrown it out. I forgot about it, and then when I remembered it, it wasn't there.

I didn't tell this story to Jessica. I told her instead about the time the cafeteria let me borrow all kinds of round fruits and vegetables so I could model the planets in orbit. Since it was made of fruit, she didn't have to ask me what happened to it after.

We got to The Coffee Tree (Sloane wasn't around) and sat down. Almost immediately, Jessica's face got serious. Like, super serious.

"So here's the thing," she said, before she'd even taken a sip. "I have no idea what you know about me, or about my family. But I'm going to tell you. My father was a raging alcoholic, emphasis on the raging. He'd beat the shit out of my brother regularly, and he would push me around without crossing the line into hitting me outright. By the time we got to middle school, my brother was taking after him. My father had this rule that nothing that happened in our house was ever to be mentioned outside of our house. My brother thought he could enforce this rule too. And I was stuck. Really stuck. Because I knew that if I told my father what my brother was doing, he'd kill my brother. I know that sounds extreme, but it *felt* extreme. You know? I didn't trust my mother to do anything. She was as stuck as I was. Then it got so bad, it couldn't be hidden anymore."

"He broke your jaw," I volunteered.

Jessica didn't look surprised. "I guess you heard that part. Everyone did. He broke my jaw. Knocked a few teeth out. Left me bleeding in my room. I sucked it up, bandaged myself up—poorly, I might add—and went to school the next day. My friends took one look at me and steered me to the school nurse. I told her I'd fallen down the stairs. And she looked at me and said, 'Do the stairs have a name?' And that did it. I don't know why. Maybe because my friends were there and they clearly weren't buying my story. Maybe because the nurse had given me an opening that nobody else had given me before. But that was it. Moment of revelation. I told her what happened. She called the counselor. He asked me if there was anyone I could think of who could help, and I gave him my aunt's number. My mother's sister. The strongest woman I could think of. And when they called her to tell her what had happened, she wasn't surprised. She didn't doubt me for a second. She came right away. And the next thing I knew, my mother and I were living in her guest room. Mom on the bed, me on an inflatable mattress. My brother was sent away to a boarding school, and he's better now. Or at least he sounds better. Whenever we see each other, it's awkward."

Jessica stopped. Looked at me. Continued.

"This is what I want to say to you, Ezra. This is why I want you to know where I'm coming from. Because I have some idea of what you're up against. Maybe not in the same way. But similar. Am I right?"

I nodded.

"So here's what I've learned. One: There's no point in hiding what's happened to you, because other people's mistreatment of you is their shame, not yours. Two: We are in a club we never wanted to belong to, the club of people who've had someone actively try to break us, and who discovered our strength in surviving. We have to reach out to each other whenever we can. And three: Whenever you're in the worst place, there is always a better place. Your abuser will try to hide it from you, but other people can help you get there. Like Terrence. Or his parents. Or your sister. She knows what she's doing."

Words failed me, Bea. All I could say was "Yes." And then again: *"Yes."*

What overwhelmed me at that moment—what's overwhelming me now as I'm writing this—wasn't just the recognition, the understanding. It was even larger than that. Because not only was I connecting to what she was saying, I was connecting to the way she was saying it. The past tense. I was thinking of what you and I went through in the past tense. All the things that happened to us—they are no longer *happening*. They *happened.* And that doesn't guarantee anything, and it doesn't erase all the pain our lives have had, but it also feels like we've proven that stories can change. The story we're telling now isn't the story we were given, the story we were forced to have. We've reached the better page.

I told Jessica all this. She nodded and chimed in and understood, really understood. Finally, she asked, "So what are you going to do?" A question I might not have been able to answer before. But now, I had an answer. I have an answer.

This is what I want to tell you:

I'm going to stay, Bea.

I'm going to stay, and then I'm going to leave.

I'm going to finish out this year. I'm going to rely on the kindness of Terrence's parents. I'm going to avoid our house, our mother, our stepfather. I'm going to wrap things up and lay the groundwork to keep Terrence and Jessica and a few others in my life.

Then I'm coming to you, Bea. I'm coming.

You're the only family I have. You're the only family I want.

I don't know how we're going to do it, but I know we're going to do it.

You'll go to college. I'll still go to high school. Somehow, we'll make the life we were never given, and be the people we want to be.

I'm hitting send now.

I'll call you in a few minutes.

Here's to the future.

Ez

Acknowledgments

Much like Ezra and Bea, we could not have done this alone.

Big heartfelt thanks to our brilliant, incomparable agents and comrades on this journey, Kerry Sparks and Bill Clegg. As well as our *Take Me with You When You Go* book home, Penguin Random House—including Melanie Nolan, our editor, as well as Barbara Marcus, Judith Haut, Emily Harburg, Jake Eldred, Arely Guzmán, Dominique Cimina, Mary McCue, Jillian Vandall, Morgan Maple, Barbara Perris, Janet Renard, Nancee Adams, Artie Bennett, Ray Shappell, Alison Kolani, John Adamo, Caitlin Whalen, Megan Mitchell, Kelly McGauley, Jules Kelly, Janine Perez, Elizabeth Ward, Jenn Inzetta, Kate Keating, Whitney Aaronson, Adrienne Waintraub, Kristin Schulz, Pam White, Jocelyn Lange, Lauren Morgan, and Catherine Kramer.

Thank you also to the incredible Tito Merello for the beautiful cover. And to Ben Horslen and the amazing team at Penguin Random House UK for being our UK home.

Thank you as well to Sylvie Rabineau and Anna DeRoy of WME for believing in us and our story.

And oh the gratitude for Janet Geddis and Avid Books, as well as the Book Loft of Amelia Island, Florida, Once Upon a Bookseller in Saint Marys, Georgia, and Mitchell Kaplan's Books & Books in Miami. Not to mention Little City Books, Books of Wonder, and every other indie bookshop, bookseller, teacher, and librarian on this planet. We can't do what we do without you. You are our heroes.

We are fortunate enough to be blessed with wonderful families and friends, who offer constant support, encouragement, inspiration, and love.

Jennifer is eternally grateful for her husband and forever-first reader, Justin Conway, for being her person, her best, and her home. And to her kids and her literary cats—Rumi, Scout, Linus, Luna, Kevin, Zelda, and Roo, and the late great Lulu, prettiest soul kitty who ever lived. Writing is not the same without Queen Lulu sitting by Jennifer's side (or on the keyboard) and yawning at the screen.

Jennifer is also grateful for her beloved family, especially Bill Niven, surrogate dad, granddad, and kitty whisperer, and sister-cousin Lisa von Sprecken (tots and taters!). For her honorary brothers, Angelo Surmelis and Joe Kraemer, and honorary sisters, Ronni Davis, Kerry Kletter, Lisa Brucker, Beth Jennings White, Grecia Reyes, and Kami Garcia. For her early readers and their invaluable feedback—Adriana Mather, Annalise von Sprecken, Kenzie Vanacore, and Lila Vanacore. For the remarkable Kenzie, Lila, and Violeta Morales Fakih, whom Jennifer is lucky enough to work with on a regular basis. For Adriana Mather, James Bird, Jeff Zentner, Emily Henry, Brittany Cavallaro, Kerry Kletter, Angelo Surmelis, Danielle Paige, and their cherished kinship. And for Claudia Dane-Stroud, Patrick Dane, and Aaron Dane for home-cooked dinners, friendship, and kitty love. And for Angelica Carbajal and Stacy Monticello for being such bright places.

Infinite thanks to Jennifer's parents, Penelope Niven and Jack F. McJunkin Jr., for all they mean to her, on this earth and beyond. For teaching her to believe in herself. For teaching her she is limitless. For boundless, unconditional love, which still surrounds her, even though they are no longer here. *I love you more than words.*

David is writing his acknowledgments at his father's desk, while his mom is in the kitchen, calling to him that the cardinal is at the bird feeder. This feels exactly right. The fact that all the pieces in his life fit so well is entirely because of them. He's also very happy to think of his dad smiling at the publication of this book; Dad was very happy to hear about it when it started—because David was so excited to write with Jennifer, and also because David finally, *finally* collaborated with someone whose last name came after his alphabetically.

As is often the case with David, a good amount of this book was written with other people in the room, often themselves writing. So thanks to Billy Merrell, Nick Eliopulos, Zack Clark, Andrew Eliopulos, Nico Medina, Anica Rissi, Mike Ross, Ben Lindsay, Caleb Huett, Elizabeth Eulberg, Justin Weinberger, and the purveyors of coffee at Think and City of Saints. Thanks, too, to everyone at Scholastic.

Finally, Jennifer and David would like to express their profound gratitude to their readers. You mean more to us than words can truly say.

Authors' Note and Resources

Too many young people are struggling in silence. If you or someone you love is suffering from abuse, please reach out, speak up.

You matter and you are not alone. Help is out there.

HOTLINES/WEBSITES

National Domestic Violence Hotline | thehotline.org
1-800-799-SAFE (7233) or 1-800-787-3224 (TTY)

Childhelp National Child Abuse Hotline | childhelp.org
1-800-4-A-CHILD (1-800-422-4453)

NO MORE | nomore.org

LGBT National Help Center | glbtnationalhelpcenter.org

VictimConnect | victimconnect.org

WomensLaw | womenslaw.org

Match Group | mtch.com/safety-details-international

Futures Without Violence | futureswithoutviolence.org

Women Against Abuse | womenagainstabuse.org

Love Is Respect | loveisrespect.org

Hotline: 1-866-331-9474

That's Not Cool | thatsnotcool.com/?ref=logo

The National Coalition Against Domestic Violence (NCADV) | ncadv.org

Helpful page: NCADV's Personalized Safety Plan

ncadv.org/personalized-safety-plan

Mission statement:

The National Coalition Against Domestic Violence (NCADV)'s mission is to lead, mobilize, and raise our voices to support efforts that demand a change of conditions that lead to domestic violence such as patriarchy, privilege, racism, sexism, and classism. We are dedicated to supporting survivors and holding offenders accountable and supporting advocates.

The blog: ncadv.org/blog

INSTAGRAM/SOCIAL MEDIA

NO MORE | instagram.com/nomoreorg

The National Coalition Against Domestic Violence | instagram.com/ncadv

Joyful Heart Foundation | instagram.com/thejhf

Love Is Respect | instagram.com/loveisrespectofficial

RESOURCES/WHERE TO LEARN MORE

Youth.Gov | youth.gov

The National Child Traumatic Stress Network | nctsn.org

American Academy of Child & Adolescent Psychiatry | aacap.org

Additional: *Trauma and Child Abuse Resource Center*

aacap.org/AACAP/Families_and_Youth/Resource_Centers/Child_Abuse_Resource_Center/Home.aspx